The Thirteen Days of Christmas

Beverly Lein

PORTLAND • OREGON
INKWATERPRESS.COM

This is a work of fiction. The events described here are imaginary. The settings and characters are fictitious and do not represent specific places or living or dead people. Any resemblance is entirely coincidental.

Copyright © 2009 by Beverly Lein

Cover designed by Masha Shubin

Interior designed by Tricia Sgrignoli/Positive Images

Cover photos © JupiterImages Corporation

Interior photo © BigStockPhoto.com, Dragut Vasile Adrian, "Santa and His Sleigh"

All rights reserved. No part of this book may be reproduced or transmitted in any form or by any means whatsoever, including photocopying, recording or by any information storage and retrieval system, without written permission from the publisher and/or author. Contact Inkwater Press at 6750 SW Franklin Street, Suite A, Portland, OR 97223-2542. 503.968.6777

www.inkwaterpress.com

ISBN-10 1-59299-441-5
ISBN-13 978-1-59299-441-0

Publisher: Inkwater Press

Printed in the U.S.A.

All paper is acid free and meets all ANSI standards for archival quality paper.

Dedicated to Barry Jonson, Brodie's Daddy, who passed away Thursday, August 13, 2009.

To my original editor Michelle Dwyer, who took the first draft and turned it into a readable story. With her calm and loving nature she guided me and the story unfolded beautifully.

To Dianne Smyth, my proofreader, friend, and editor: Thank you for all your wisdom and your faith in me.

Most of all, my grandchildren who helped me write this story: Brittany, Morgan, Sydnee, Rachel, and Ashley. With you all reading the chapters and adding adventures, it was so much fun. Especially Sydnee – who thought I should rewrite and add her dad to the story, making it a better and exciting story.

Thank you.
With all my love,

Mostly known as Grandma Bev

Beverly Lein

The snow, driven by a frenzied wind, swirled around the cabin. A lone window shed light out into the darkness and a small face stared out into the night. The falling temperature had bothered the little girl and she hoped that the animals in the barn wouldn't freeze. She could no longer see the barn and she was pretty sure the temperature had fallen to 50 degrees below zero Celsius, which wasn't uncommon for northern Alberta in this winter of 1866. The inside of the cabin was cosy if you were near the fire, but away from it the cold had begun to seep into the corners.

Brittany looked around at the sleeping forms of her little brother and the three little girls who were her cousins. She stood admiring nine-year-old Morgan with his dark eyelashes and hair, which created a startling contrast against the white pillowcase. Brittany could never get over how cute her little brother was.

The little girls were darlings as well. Sydnee, who was eight, had long dark blonde hair that hung to her waist and perfectly set blue-green eyes. Six-year-old Rachel, with eyes like her sister's, had her mother Lana's white-blonde hair and soft porcelain skin. Her hair was much shorter than Sydnee's because Rachel had decided to give herself a haircut. Her mother had been horrified, left with no alternative but to cut it again to even it out. It had already grown out quite a bit and was now just reaching her shoulders. And then there was three-year-old Ashley, the apple of everyone's eye, with her short golden curls and wide-set blue-green eyes. She was as adorable as they come and with her unique personality, she had everyone wrapped around her little finger. The furry blankets were keeping the little ones warm and unaware of the storm raging outside.

For the last two weeks 11-year-old Brittany had tried to smother the fear that overwhelmed her as she wondered what had happened to her parents. They had left her to look after the little ones while they made the daylong trip to North Star for Christmas supplies. Christmas was just a month away and Darren and Alison had wanted to make the 45-mile trip early in the month. They had planned to take the three little girls, who were their nieces, to see their mother, Lana, before Christmas. The girls had already been with them for the month of November and Alison was worried that they were getting homesick. The plan had been to take Sydnee, Rachel, and Ashley to see their mother in North Star and then bring them back home with them. Lana would arrive later, just before Christmas, and spend the holidays with them at the cabin.

As they prepared for the trip to town the weather had remained bitterly cold. Brittany always hated making the long cold trip to town and she had begged them to let her and the other children stay home. "Mom, why can't we stay home?" she pleaded. "I know how to milk the cow and do the chores. I could babysit the little kids and I know how to cook. Come on, Mom. Don't make us go on that cold trip!"

"The girls are homesick for their mom and she's probably really missing them by now," Alison replied. "Besides, Brittany, you're still pretty young to be left alone with four little kids."

"But, Mom, I've watched them all day lots of times when you've gone hunting with Dad or worked in the fields all day. What difference is three days? And, it's only two-and-a-half days when you hurry!"

Alison looked lovingly at her serious young daughter. Brittany's large black eyes were so much like her little brother's, and her long dark brown hair cascaded down to her waist. She was a beautiful child, tall for her years, and if you didn't know how old she was, you might think she was around 15 or 16.

"Okay," Alison sighed, "I'll talk it over with your dad and we'll see. I'm not promising anything though."

Brittany hugged her mom. "Thanks, Mom; I know we'll all be happier at home."

The little girls and Morgan, who had been listening to this conversation, now chimed in, "Please, Auntie!" assuring her that they would be good and that they'd help Brittany.

Alison looked at their sincere little faces. They all burst out laughing when Ashley said, "Me help too, Auntie!" Everyone knew Ashley's determination to help usually ended up making extra work for everyone.

As Alison worked she thought about Brittany. Brittany had been born an "old soul." And, in some way, the other children seemed aware of this trait in Brittany. They never questioned her authority when she was looking after them. Alison's mind wandered farther away as she started to think about Grandma Bev and Grandpa Carson. "Poppa," Ashley had named him when she first began to talk, and the others soon began to call him that too. Alison missed her mother-in-law. They had all lived close together at first, but then Darren and Alison had found this place and moved further into the wilderness.

Lana had moved with them but now lived in the town of North Star, where she could make a living for herself and her little girls. Bev and Carson remained in Peace River, another 60 miles from North Star. Alison was pretty sure that her in-laws were going to move to North Star in the spring because they missed their grandchildren and the kids missed them dreadfully. Alison had hoped that they would all be together for Christmas. She mused about how Grandma Bev had names for all of her grandchildren that perfectly described their different personalities. Brittany was her Old Soul – Grandma Bev had been the first to recognize this. Sydnee was her Shiny Star because she was always so interested in the stars and the Northern Lights in the winter. Rachel was the Good Granddaughter. She had given her that name when Rachel had told her, "Grandma, you're a good grandma." Ashley was Rainbow because when she was born her sisters had wanted to name her Rainbow. Morgan was nicknamed the Informer, as he was always busy informing everyone on what all the girls were up to.

Alison smiled as she thought about her husband. Darren stood six feet tall, a big man with dark brown eyes and sandy blond hair. His nature was easy going and gentle. In contrast, Alison was petite and had black eyes. They made a handsome couple and complemented each other very well.

When Darren came home that night he and Alison discussed the idea of leaving the children home on their own. "You know, Alison," Darren said, "that might not be a bad idea. It is 40 below and it looks like this cold snap's going to hang on for a while. We would only be gone for two-and-a-half days and Brittany does handle things very well. We could get our shopping done in no time and the kids wouldn't be freezing their little bottoms off. The little girls don't seem to be all that homesick for their mom yet. We'll talk it over with the kids in the morning and if they really want to stay home, maybe we'll let them."

At breakfast Darren asked Brittany, "Do you think you can handle the chores and the little ones on your own?"

"Sure I can, Dad! Morgan and Sydnee can do a lot to help. They're good at carrying wood – they do it all the time for Mom. I have it all planned out. I can milk the cow early in the morning and then after breakfast we can all go outside and do the rest of the chores together. Just make sure you chop lots of wood for us. I hate chopping wood."

Alison knew there was plenty of canned moose meat, chicken, and meatballs, and lots of vegetables. To prepare an evening meal Brittany would only need to peel potatoes and open up jars of canned meat and vegetables. Getting supper wouldn't be too hard. There was always oatmeal and milk for breakfast and she would bake extra bread for lunches before they left, just in case they were delayed. She could even freeze some outside. So that afternoon and evening Alison baked eight loaves and froze six of them, just in case.

The next morning, December 2, was a beautiful, crisp, cold day and Darren and Alison set out on their journey. The temperature was hovering at 30 degrees below zero as the kids waved goodbye, excited to be without grownups for a day or two. Alison called out last-minute instructions, "Make sure you bundle up well when you go outside, bar the door at night, and don't wander too far from the cabin when you go out to play." The children watched until Darren and Alison were out of sight and then scurried back into the warmth of the cabin, thankful that they didn't have to be travelling in the cold.

❄   ❄   ❄

Gabriel made his way through the deep snow, pulling his robe tightly around his big frame. It was a cold day and it was a good thing he didn't have much farther to go. Nearing the North Pole, he raised his arms and Santa's mystical village came into view. It was a quaint village with white snow covering everything and crystal icicles hanging from the eaves and the trees. The cottage-style workshops stood in a large circle in rows at least half-a-mile long. There were eight rows and around the perimeter of each were about a thousand little cottages with crystal-like icicles hanging from their eaves. In the centre of the village stood a two-storey house with four gables and dormer windows overlooking each part of the village. Frost covered the windows, making it hard to see through the panes and a heavy hoar frost covered the surrounding trees with sparkly silver snow. All the buildings were brown with white trim, except for Santa's house, which was white with brown trim.

Beside Santa's house were a huge barn and a field where reindeer roamed freely. Elfin children were everywhere frolicking with the animals and taking rides on their backs. Reindeer flew magically through the air with little ones on their backs. The only rule for the children riding the reindeer was that they weren't allowed to fly too high up in the air or leave the fairy-tale perimeter of the village.

The elves were dressed in red and green attire, their bubbly personalities radiating love and happiness. One and all, their job was to fill the world with love, happiness, and peace.

Their world was safe, but they all knew that outside in the real world there was a lot of unhappiness. They knew that children suffered, adults didn't always get along, many people were poor, and some of them didn't have enough food. They knew that sometimes families didn't stay together because of problems of their own making, while others were torn apart through no fault of their own. Sometimes bad things happened to good people and they knew that it was the job of Santa, with the help of the elves, to try to make life a little happier and to bring peace to people all over the world.

As Gabriel approached Santa's house, joy filled his heart. He always loved coming here though this time it was different. He had been sent from the heavenly realm of God to enlist the help of Santa. Saint Joseph had also been summoned to return to the earth where there was a family in great need of help. The Holy Father had said that it would take all three of them to save and reunite this little family.

Santa opened the door before Gabriel could knock and the two old friends hugged each other in greeting, each being very glad to see the other. "Gabriel, what brings you here? I haven't seen you in ages! Come in. Come in. Warm yourself. Have some hot cocoa and we'll talk while you rest." From the red-brick fireplace came the sound of a fire crackling and snapping. Two old leather chairs were pulled close to the warmth of the hearth.

Mrs. Claus hurried into the room bringing the hot drinks. Setting them down, she hugged Gabriel and said, "What a wonderful surprise! Welcome back to the North Pole."

Once Gabriel had settled into his chair he explained to his two old friends about the family in need and what was about to take place. "I know this is a very busy time of the year for you, Nicholas, but your help is urgently needed."

Nicholas reached out and patted Gabriel's arm saying, "We're never too busy to help but I hope it's not too late. What is the nature of the problem?" Gabriel explained that Saint Joseph was going to help as well.

"Where is he now and will he make it here before we have to leave? We'll be leaving soon, you know," noted Santa.

"He is already on the job," replied Gabriel. "We'll all meet together when the time is right. But we must hurry – this misfortune has already begun to unfold."

❄ ❄ ❄

As Darren and Alison waved goodbye to the children, Alison was uneasy and felt sad deep down. "You know, Darren, I still don't feel right about leaving them by themselves."

Darren reached over and squeezed her hand saying, "We'll be back before you have time to miss them. They're so proud of being treated as young adults and they're all pretty capable kids, except Ashley of course, so I don't think they will have any trouble outside of a scrap or two."

Banjo, their laid-back old horse, pulled the sleigh through the considerable snowfall without too much trouble. When they came to a deep drift Darren would jump off the sleigh and help the horse pull until they were safely through it. So far, they had made very good time and were about 15 miles from town when they approached a steep grade that would take them down a winding snow-laden trail to the bottom of the little valley and into the town. As they started down, Darren pulled back on the reins so they wouldn't get going too fast around the corners that were coming quickly to meet them.

When they reached the third turn they didn't even notice the mountain lion that was crouched on the ledge above them.

The cat had been stalking them for the last few miles, waiting for an opportune moment to attack. Usually the big cats didn't pick such a healthy animal as the large horse pulling the sleigh, but he had been watching long enough to notice that at times the horse would flounder in the deep snow. The mountain lion had recently hurt his hind leg and because of this food had been scarce for a few days. By this time hunger had taken over and his animal instincts told him that he had to eat and he had immediately sensed that the horse might be easy pickings. As the horse and sleigh began to approach the area under the ledge he made his leap, landing awkwardly on Banjo's back.

Banjo reared up in shock and desperation when the lion landed on him. Darren raised the whip and struck out at the big cat. The whip wrapped itself around the lion's neck. The horse jerked sideways, lost his footing and went over the cliff, taking the sleigh and Darren and Alison with him. The sleigh with the four of them rolled over and over for about 200 feet and finally came to rest at the bottom. All was quiet as the snow swirled around the dead horse and the mountain lion, which still had the whip wrapped around its neck. The young couple lay about 30 feet from one another, both knocked unconscious. Snow began to fall gently and soon covered their broken bodies.

When the fourth day arrived Brittany started to fret. Where could her parents be? They should have returned home by now. The novelty of being the adult and of playing house was beginning to wear off. Everyone was pulling his or her weight, but Morgan was starting to miss his mom. Of course when the little girls heard him crying for his mom they would begin to cry for theirs. To make matters worse, Ashley wouldn't just cry and ask for her mom, she wanted her Uma and Poppa too. Brittany carried her around, trying to comfort her and trying hard not to cry herself.

The food Alison had prepared had been eaten and they were almost out of chopped wood. Brittany added making meals and chopping wood to her list. She got the little ones to pack the smaller pieces of wood into the house while she split the larger blocks. Thank goodness there were plenty of potatoes and cans of meat, vegetables, and fruit in the cellar.

The weather was getting colder and the fireplace required more and more wood to keep the cabin warm. Between milking the cow, hauling melted snow water to the animals in the barn, and packing snow into the wooden barrels inside the cabin, Brittany's job was becoming more and more overwhelming. Once the outside work was done she cleaned the cabin, made the meals, and cared for the little ones. Each one helped but someone had to organize everything and that responsibility lay heavily on Brittany's shoulders. As the days passed with no sign of her parents, Brittany became more troubled, crying herself to sleep at night, trying not to let the little ones see the fear that had taken over her.

❄ ❄ ❄

In town a slender young woman with lovely shoulder-length blonde hair and blue eyes put the final touches on the young man's haircut. She then swept up the hair that had fallen to the floor while the young lad fished in his pocket for the 50 cents he owed her. She watched him leave the shop and then turned her attention to the stove, filling the firebox with wood.

She had made this side of the large room into a little diner. Four tables were covered in red tablecloths, with four chairs placed neatly at each table. A long table held her pies, biscuits, and other baked goods. On the stove, a huge pot of chicken stew simmered, filling the place with its savoury aroma. A hutch stood nearby with dishes and cutlery where people could take a plate and fill it with food before sitting down. Cups also hung from the hutch, enabling the customers to fill them with coffee, tea, or water. Alongside the stove stood the huge wood box and four wooden barrels with melted snow water.

A large bowl of stew with a biscuit and coffee would cost a customer 75 cents; a piece of pie was 10 cents; and a cookie or piece of cake, a nickel. Between running the diner and cutting hair, Lana managed to make a living for herself and her children.

Lana had bought the large old building from a businessman in town. She had gotten it cheap because it needed a lot of work. The man had agreed to let her make a $10 payment every month, or $120 a year. With her father's help she had fixed up the front part of the building for her business. He had planned to work to make the large back room into living quarters for her and the children. Unfortunately, he had fallen off a ladder and suffered a severe leg fracture. He had returned home to let his leg mend and Lana was left in the lurch, as she couldn't afford to hire anyone to do the carpentry required to fix the back room. Her brother Darren and sister-in-law Alison had taken her little girls to give her time to get her business up and running. Without a living area, or the money to rent a place, she knew the girls were better off in her brother's home for the time being.

Lana sighed as she thought of her precious little girls. She missed them so much. She was hoping to go to Darren's on December 23 and spend Christmas with the family. Perhaps she would be in a position to bring her little ones home with her afterwards. It was already the 10th of December and she still had no one to help her finish the renovations. It would be heartbreaking to go to them at Christmas and then have to leave them behind because she still had no home for them. Lana frowned to herself; something else was bothering her. Alison had told her that they would be coming to town for Christmas supplies in the early part of December. They planned on bringing the children with them to see her for a day or two, but she still had not heard from them. It had been so cold – perhaps they hadn't travelled into town after all – but still it was getting late into the month.

Lana knew that her brother worried about her and felt sorry for her. She worked hard and without a husband so many things got left undone. Darren and Alison lived so far away and with farming and trapping, their life was tough too. The only help he could offer was to take her babies, God bless him.

Lana hung her head and a sob escaped as she looked down at her red chapped hands. She gave haircuts and served food all day, hauling in snow and chopping wood between customers. Behind the building she raised her own chickens for eggs and butchering. She bought beef and pork from farmers. At night she baked her pies, cakes, biscuits, and cookies and readied her hearty soups or stews for the next day. The last thing she did each night was pack in snow to fill the large wooden barrels so that she would have plenty of water for the next day. She found chopping firewood the most difficult chore and as soon as the huge wood box was filled for the night, she fell into bed exhausted. Having no bedroom, she'd pull her small cot out from the cold back quarters where the wind blew in through cracks in the walls. She'd fall asleep exhausted and then be up again by five the next morning, readying herself for the day by pushing her bed into the back room and dressing beside the warm fire.

As she wiped the tears away, she saw an old man leading a donkey toward her shop. He tied the animal to the railing, the cold wind whipping his raggedy cloak about him. Snow had piled up on his worn felt hat – a hat that had probably once been grand but was now shiny from use. When he came through the door Lana could see that his brown beard was streaked with grey and had little icicles hanging from it. His appearance was frightening until one looked into his eyes. They were kind and gentle, calming.

"Hello, child," he said. "May I come in and warm myself by your fire?"

"Oh, yes!" Lana replied as she hurried over to help him remove his old cloak. The old man's gaze went to the stew pot from which the aroma of food wafted into the air.

"I have no money but I am very hungry. If you will feed me, I'll chop wood or do whatever chores I can."

"Never mind, sir," Lana said, "Come, sit down. A bowl of stew will neither make me nor break me and I will not have anyone go hungry."

"What is your name, child?" the old man asked.

Lana told him her name as she filled a bowl with stew. She handed him the bowl, which he took over to one of the tables. Bringing coffee for both of them, as well as biscuits and a napkin, she sat down beside him.

As he ate, Lana inquired, "What's your name?"

Stopping to wipe his mouth, he responded with great pride, "My name is Joseph. I have travelled many miles looking for work, but there aren't too many jobs to be had at this time of the year. Most men are at home now and they do their own work."

"What sort of work is it that you do, Joseph?" Lana asked.

"I'm a carpenter by trade."

Tears appeared in Lana's eyes. "You're a carpenter! Oh, my God, that is exactly what I've been praying for!" Words bubbled out of her mouth as she told the old man her sad story. She finished by telling him that in another two weeks she could go get her babies, but that she still didn't have a home for them.

Joseph reached across the table and took her red chapped hands in his and squeezed them gently. "Well, my dear, for free meals and a place to sleep I will do all your chores if you will give me the job."

"Oh, yes!" Lana said, "And if I have any free time, I will help you." Then a frown flickered across her face.

"Is there a problem? I can see you are disturbed."

Lana confided, "I'm worried about my brother and sister-in-law. They told me they were going to make a trip into town at the beginning of this month and bring the children to see me. They haven't come yet. I realize that it's been bitterly cold, but even if they decided not to bring the children, I would have thought that Darren would make the trip on his own."

A sad look crossed Joseph's face and he said, "Well, child, let's work hard and see what we can get done in the next two weeks. If no one shows up at the end of a week-and-a-half, maybe you can make arrangements to head out there earlier than you had planned. You did say you were to go there for Christmas, didn't you?"

"Oh, yes!" said Lana, "And maybe you can come spend Christmas with us too and meet my brother and his wife and all our wonderful children. You have nowhere else to go, do you, Joseph?"

"No, child," the old man replied quietly, "My place is with you for now."

Joseph worked hard and Lana marvelled at the beautiful work he did. It seemed that whatever he built or fixed came alive. He packed wood shavings into the walls for insulation and soon the cold wind was unable to blow through the cracks. Even without heat the room had warmed up enough to work comfortably without his hands freezing.

Joseph watched the young woman working day and night without much rest. Sunday was the only day she didn't open her shop, but after church she worked quickly to do all the extra chores that she couldn't get done during the week. She washed her clothes, napkins, and tablecloths, and filled the big tub with water so that they could both have a weekly bath. She settled for sponge baths through the week but looked forward to a long soak in the tub each Saturday night – the only pampering time she ever got.

On Sunday afternoons Lana used her extra time to ready food for the next week. She usually butchered a couple of chickens and prepared for the stew pot as well as enough baking for a couple of days. What a blessing it was to have Joseph nearby. He saved her hours of work by chopping wood and hauling snow in to melt for water. Whenever he chopped wood he added extra to the pile. Soon there was more wood in the chopped pile than there was in the not-chopped pile. Lana thought perhaps it would be a good idea to hire someone to chop her wood next year when they delivered it.

The back room was taking on a personality of its own. Now it consisted of two large bedrooms, a huge pantry, a utility room to wash clothes, and a bathroom with a big tub and a toilet. The toilet had a seat and a lid to close over the slop pail, which was tucked in below and emptied every day. Lana had never seen anything like it. How nice it would be for her and the little girls not to have to go outside in the cold and dark to the outhouse. The big bathtub had a drain that went down under the floor. Once the plug was pulled the water ran on its own outside under the house without anyone having to empty it by pails.

The kitchen and living room were combined with a fireplace in the centre. Joseph made the fireplace so that it would warm all the rooms at the same time. The fireplace that faced the living room and kitchen was open. Lana had never seen one built like that. It was wonderful.

But as the days went by and Darren and Alison didn't appear, Lana's heart became heavier and heavier. Something was wrong; she just felt it in her soul.

Because of Joseph's help with the heavier chores, Lana now had time to spend making Christmas gifts. She knit matching sweaters, toques, and scarves for Darren and Alison. For the children she crocheted little sweaters, socks, and mitts with matching wool. She made doll clothes to fit the homemade dolls she had made for the little girls. She decided that only a new robe would do for Joseph. She went to the store and brought a huge piece of cowhide, cut it to size, and lined the inside with crocheted wool. Down the front she made buttonholes and sewed on buttons. She crocheted heavy wool socks and made beautiful moccasins with the leftover hide. Now the old man would never be as cold as when she had first seen him.

Lana hurried to get everything ready for the trip, packing food and candies, and wrapping the presents. She wanted to have everything ready by December 20th so she could start the journey to her brother's. This was earlier than she had planned to leave, but she could no longer wait. Worry for her family was eating at her heart. Darren *always* came to town before Christmas unless someone was hurt or sick.

Lana had made plans to rent a horse and sleigh for the journey. Joseph decided to travel on his donkey. She was so grateful that he was coming with her. Lana was growing to love the gentle old man and hoped he would never leave. She intended to ask him to stay after Christmas and make his home with her and the little girls. If he could help with the chores and the children, she knew she could make enough money to support him as well as her family. He was so handy at everything he did, but most of all, he was patient with her and kind to everyone who came into the shop.

❆ ❆ ❆

Carson was angry and worried sick about Lana and the little girls. Laid up with a badly broken leg, he was making life miserable for his wife. He knew that Darren would help his sister as much as he could, but they lived so far apart and winter didn't make it easy for Darren to get to Lana. Carson didn't know that Darren had taken the children to live with him and his good little wife. Bev, Carson's wife, couldn't leave him to go to help their daughter because she had to care for him. He knew how she felt though because he could hear her crying in the night. He didn't know if she was crying for Lana or the little girls – probably for all of them.

At 60, Carson was a good-looking man with greying hair, but he was beginning to feel a lot of aches and pains. He had broken his leg at the end of August and it was mending slowly, very slowly. As he was lying in bed with morning approaching, he could hear his wife in the kitchen making breakfast. He had a good wife, he thought, one he probably didn't deserve. She constantly had to hush him up because he complained a lot and worried about everything. As he listened to the familiar sounds coming from the kitchen, he thought about his wife. Bev was an attractive and vivacious woman with dark brown eyes that ignited when she was mad. Her flashing dark eyes were generally used in reaction to him more than anyone else. He knew how to push her buttons all right. And when he did all hell would break loose, but she loved him dearly and looked after him well. She was a good mother and missed the grandchildren terribly, especially the baby, Ashley. They had planned to move to North Star this fall but he had broken his leg and now they would have to wait until spring.

Bev came to the bedroom door and said, "Breakfast is ready. Do you need help getting up?"

"No, I can manage," he said as he pulled himself out of the bed. Once they were sitting at the breakfast table he inquired, "Mother, how would you feel about making the long trip to the kids' for Christmas?"

Jumping up from her chair so fast she knocked it over, Bev gasped, "Oh, Carson! Could we? Oh, please! For sure?" Hugging him around the neck, she said, "Do you think your leg is well enough to travel that far?"

"I think so, but we should ask Morgan's young friend Brodie if he will come with us. He could help drive the team and do a lot of running for us. He's strong and smart for his age and he would probably like to see Morgan. We will leave on the 22nd and it should take us about two days to get to Lana's. Then we'll travel with her and the little girls to Darren's."

It being the 20th already, Bev gave him a gentle slap on the back and said, "Trust you to leave it to the last minute to make up your mind! You go talk to Brodie and see if he will come with us. I have a lot of shopping to do and things to get ready in just a short time."

❄ ❄ ❄

Darren regained consciousness with pain wracking his body. Lying still for a few moments, afraid to move, he tried to figure out where he was and why he was lying outside in the snow. As the memory washed over him, he struggled to get up. "Oh, my God! Alison, where are you?" he hollered as he rolled over, getting up on his knees. He gagged as pain pierced his ribcage. He must have broken or cracked his ribs – they hurt so badly he could hardly breathe. Nausea overtook him completely. He realized his leg was broken as well so he stayed in a sitting position. Grabbing a nearby tree, he pulled himself to his feet gasping and fighting the blackness that tried to overtake him. Blood was still trickling down his face from a cut on the side of his head. He had been knocked out, but had no idea for how long – an hour or two by the looks of the darkening winter sky.

Groggily looking around he finally spotted Alison, the snow almost covering her quiet body. His heart pounding, hardly daring to breathe, Darren lumbered his way over to his wife, dragging his broken leg. Clutching at his ribcage, trying to apply pressure to his side, he reached his wife. He dropped down into the snow beside her and gathered her into his arms. Tears running down his face, he felt for a pulse. "Please, God, let her be alive," he prayed. She was breathing, but she had a terrible lump on her forehead in the form of a hoof print. Old Banjo had somehow hit her or kicked her as they rolled down the cliff. The position of her arm told him it was broken and her awkwardly bent leg told even more. He wouldn't know how badly it was broken until he made some sort of shelter and a fire so he could undress her. Pulling her with him he dragged himself back to the upset sleigh. Everything that had been in the sleigh was scattered far and wide. Getting Alison to the sleigh took nearly every ounce of strength he had left in him, but he had much to do before he could lie down again to rest. He managed to reach one of the blankets and wrapped it tightly around Alison.

Pulling himself up, he began to gather things that had fallen out of the sleigh. If it was too far away or wasn't needed for immediate use, he left it lying in the snow. Unsheathing the knife at his waist, he crawled over to Banjo and started to skin the horse. He needed the horse's hide to make a shelter. Two hours later he had wrestled off the hide. Next, he turned to the big cat that lay close beside the horse and began to remove its hide as well. Crawling under the sleigh, he pulled the hides in after him, placing the bloody side down in the snow. Carefully, he pulled his wife's cold body under the sleigh, all the while groaning with pain and fighting for consciousness. Once he had her inside he covered her with the rest of the blankets from the sleigh.

He had to make it warm or they would freeze to death before morning so he struggled back outside and crawled to a large pine tree and began hacking off boughs. He cut as many as he could. Making trip after trip to the sleigh, he covered the sleigh, piling branches densely so that the cold wind couldn't penetrate. When he was satisfied, he crawled around gathering enough deadwood and branches to make a fire and keep it going through the night. His last job was to find the billycan they carried in the sleigh for making coffee and fill it with snow. Pulling wood inside, he piled it close to where he would lie down once he was settled. He built a fire in front of the small opening he had left to allow the smoke to go outside. The fire was close enough to him that he could reach his stash of wood and feed the fire through the night. He laid his rifle nearby, as there was no doubt the dead horse would draw predators.

Finally, he rested his pain-filled body beside his wife's, pulling the blanket and hide around their bodies. He wrapped his arms around her cold little frame, trying to warm her body with his. There was no use trying to set her bones tonight – not only was it too dark – his body hurt so badly he couldn't make it do another thing. As he lay there he thought that nothing had ever felt as good as when the fire started to warm his bones. His last thought before he fell into an exhausted sleep was a prayer that Alison be alive in the morning.

The cold woke Darren in the morning. The fire had gone out, but under the hides Alison's body was warm against his. Darren tried to edge away from his wife without disturbing her. As he moved, he was gripped by pain and began to vomit, retching on an empty stomach. Pain consumed his body. The heaving hurt his ribs so badly he thought he was going to die, but if he died Alison would too. Willing himself to get control, he knew the first thing he had to do was make some sort of support for his ribs. He removed his coat, then pulled off his shirt and cut it into strips. Tying the strips around his ribs made him feel better immediately, less like he was going to fall apart. He put his coat back on, then quickly built up the fire and put on the snow-filled billycan.

After cutting some of the horsemeat into small pieces, he dropped them into the boiling water to cook. He would have a little broth once the meat cooked and something for Alison when she came around. Once he had something in his stomach maybe the queasiness would disappear.

The next thing he had to do was to set his broken leg. He knew he had to help himself before he could help Alison. He crawled out from beneath the sleigh and cut some long branches from the willows for his leg and for Alison's breaks as well. Crawling over to Banjo, he cut off the reins. He could use the reins to tie around the willow branches in order to make splints so the bones couldn't move once they were pulled back into place. Wiggling his broken leg beneath the ski of the sleigh, he prepared himself to pull fast and hard so the leg would snap back into place. He knew he had to do it fast and hard because the pain would be unbearable and he wouldn't be able to do it twice. Holding his breath, he pulled as hard as he could, felt the leg pop back into place – and promptly passed out. Fifteen minutes later when he revived, he took the splints and affixed them quickly and securely around his leg. Once his leg was immobile it began to feel better and he thought that maybe he was going to live after all.

He crawled back into the shelter to his wife. In one way he was thankful that she was still unconscious as he set her arm and leg. He was finishing up when Alison started to moan. Opening her eyes, she said, "Darren, what's happening?"

"Honey, we had a really bad accident and we've been seriously injured. I just finished setting your broken bones. You must be hurting really bad."

Alison groaned again and tears ran down her cheeks as pain consumed her.

"Here, Alison, I made some broth out of old Banjo. He died in the fall. It's not that tasty, but it will warm your insides." As Darren helped Alison drink the broth and eat a few chunks of meat, his eyes kept going to the lump on her head. The way she kept closing her eyes made him fear that she had a concussion. He kept moving her a bit until he thought

The Three Saints of Christmas

she had consumed enough broth and then he gently laid her down. In no time, Alison was back in her own world where there was no pain.

That night as Darren tried to sleep, dread filled his whole being. It was now December 6th and they had been gone from home four days. He was powerless to do anything else to help his wife or himself. The children were alone in the middle of nowhere in the cold of winter. Maybe with just the broken leg he could have tried to pull himself and Alison out of the ravine, but with his broken ribs he was barely able to move, let alone trying to pack or pull her. Not a soul knew where they were and no one knew that the children were alone. The worst of it was that there was no way he could get help and if he didn't get help, his wife was going to die. Furthermore, he didn't know how much longer he could hold out. It took everything he had to gather wood.

Alison had not woken since he had given her the broth, but she seemed to be breathing without difficulty. Two more days passed, and on December 8th Darren lost consciousness as well. Eventually, the fire went out and snow began to cover the sleigh, preparing a white grave for the young couple inside.

❅ ❅ ❅

A spry old man wearing a red toque hollered at his reindeer, "Come on, boys, you can do it!" The animals pushed their way through heavy snowdrifts towards Nick's destiny and mission. "Where on earth is that sleigh?" Nick asked himself. "Gabriel said it was around here somewhere."

Finally, he sighted the sleigh with a ski still poking out from the snow. A few more days with the snow piling up against it and the ski would have been covered as well, making it virtually impossible for anyone to find it. The only blessing to the heavy snow was that it had made a warm insulation for the two people inside, keeping them from freezing to death.

Digging through the snow and clearing the boughs away, Nick could see the young couple inside. A lump formed inside of the old man's throat as he viewed the big man. He still had his arms wrapped around his wife trying to keep her warm and protect her. Nick pulled the big man out first and lifted him onto the sleigh. Covering him quickly so he didn't lose too much warmth, Nick returned to the wreck and removed Alison, leaving her wrapped in the same blankets Darren had wrapped so tightly around her. She was in serious condition, her breathing shallow. Nick knew he would have to move fast if he was to save her. Quickly he placed her on the sleigh next to her husband and covered them both with another heavy blanket.

Once they were both secure he jumped into his sleigh and hollered at the reindeer, "Up, up, and away!" The reindeer and the big sleigh lifted off the ground and flew into the air toward Nick's home. Darren, regaining consciousness for a few moments, felt like he was flying through the air and thought he must be dead or dreaming. Then he passed out once again.

Upon reaching his home, Nick worked quickly to get the young couple out of their frozen clothes and then wrapped them in warm blankets. Nick laboured over the young woman until she began to respond. His wife had brought some broth, which he gently spooned into the woman's mouth. After preparing proper casts, he replaced Darren's and then set Alison's arm and leg. Now the only thing to do was to hope that the terrible bump on her head wouldn't be her undoing.

Leaving her in his wife's capable hands, he turned his attention to the big man lying quietly in the next bed. The man's hands were badly frozen. He had worked so hard to make a shelter to save himself and his wife and obviously had been unaware of his frozen hands. Digging in the snow for wood and making the shelter cost the man dearly. Gangrene had set in and Nick knew that to save the man's hands he would have to remove two fingers from one hand and one from the other.

Nick and his wife worked around the clock on the young couple, who continued to slip in and out of consciousness. Finally, on December 16, Nick turned to his wife and said, "Ava, I think they're going to make it. Recovery is going to be slow, but I think we have moved them a few feet from death's door."

Ava went over to her husband and put her arms around him. They stood there holding each other and looking at the young couple that had so much to live for.

❄ ❄ ❄

Brittany hoped it would quit snowing by morning. She and the little kids had packed in extra wood the night before. The previous day she had split wood for two hours and her arms were aching. The chores had to be done twice a day. During the day they had to pack snow into the barrels inside the cabin so it would melt and provide enough water for the animals in the barn as well as for themselves. She then had to pack four pails of water out to the barn for the cow, calf, pigs, and chickens. In addition, the cow had to be milked twice a day. Between making meals, helping the little ones dress and bathe, keeping the cabin clean, packing in snow, and chopping wood, everything was beginning to overwhelm the young girl.

The howling blizzard and cold only added to her workload, making it harder to do the outside chores. She decided that the next day she would keep the little girls inside. Sydnee could look after them while she and Morgan worked outside. It was hard to dress the children warmly enough for the outdoors in this weather. After being outside for only 10 minutes, she would have to stop and take them inside to warm up. She and Morgan could work faster without the children delaying them, and the faster they got the outside chores done, the faster they could get inside where it was warm. Sydnee and Rachel could wash the dishes, sweep the floor, and keep the inside of the cabin clean while she and Morgan were outside.

Sometimes when she was outside the little girls would start scrapping. Most times Brittany knew how to deal with them, but at other times she would throw her hands in the air and go lie on the bed and cry. Tonight had been one of those times. But when the little girls saw how upset she was they came over to her and said they were sorry. At least that's the word the two older girls said. Ashley's version was, "I 'orry, Bitt." Of course, Brittany, who loved and worried about them all the time, hugged and kissed them, making them feel better and making herself feel better at the same time.

In the morning, Brittany noticed Morgan looking at the gun above the fireplace and said, "What's the matter, Morgan?"

"Brittany, we have to take the gun down and put it where we can reach it."

"Why?" asked Brittany.

Looking around to see where the little girls were, he whispered, "Well, yesterday I seen tracks of a mountain lion over by the shed."

Brittany shuddered with fear and nodded. Yes, the gun would have to come down. Pushing the table, which was higher than a chair, over to the fireplace, Brittany climbed up and took the gun down from the wall and handed it to her brother. Morgan knew all about guns, having gone hunting many times with his dad. He knew a gun always had to be checked to see that there were no bullets in it when not in use and never to point it at anyone. Brittany handed him the box of bullets and Morgan loaded the gun. Then they placed the gun on top of the fireplace where they could reach it easily enough, but where the little ones couldn't get to it.

Around three o'clock Brittany was chopping wood and Morgan was hauling it inside to the wood box, trying to get enough wood in for the night. Morgan stopped inside to chat with his little cousins and to warm up as he waited for Brittany to have enough wood chopped for another armful. As he opened the door to go back outside, his heart stopped in his chest. On top of the woodpile crouched a mountain lion with its tail flicking back and forth. Brittany, busily chopping wood, was oblivious to the predator above her. Morgan backed into the cabin and closed the door quietly putting a finger to his lips. The little girls knew to be very quiet by the look on his face.

Moving quickly, he pushed a chair over to the fireplace and lifted down the gun. Cocking the gun, he ran back to the door and opened it just as the big cat leaped down on Brittany. Morgan didn't even take time to aim. He just lifted the rifle and fired. Miraculously, he had hit the lion in the head and killed it, just as it landed on Brittany. The force of the big cat's landing knocked her to the ground. She struggled fiercely to get out from under the cat, but it took both Brittany pushing and Morgan pulling to get her free.

Brittany had seen the lion on top of the woodpile watching her, but she had known not to run. She had simply clutched the axe more tightly and hoped that she would at least be able to swing the axe at the lion to protect herself. Unfortunately, she didn't have a chance to swing at the cat before it jumped on her. Good thing Morgan had been there or she would be dead. Morgan and Brittany knelt in the snow, crying and holding each other. Brittany said, "Thank heaven Daddy taught you how to shoot a gun."

Brittany and Morgan hauled the dead mountain lion over to the shed. It could stay in there until Daddy came home and skinned it. The little girls joined them outside once they knew it was safe to come out. None of them had ever seen a mountain lion up close and they couldn't believe how big the cat was. Morgan was the hero of the day, but he tried to take all the praise he was getting without becoming smug. He couldn't imagine what all the fuss was about. Really, wasn't a man supposed to look after his family?

Everybody helped do the outside chores that night because the little girls were too scared to stay in the house by themselves. After they finished supper and played a few games of marbles, Brittany washed the baby and got her ready for bed. The older kids washed themselves while Brittany was tending to Ashley. When everyone was settled she read them a story and it wasn't long before the sound of quiet breathing filled the room and she knew they were all asleep.

She thought about her mom and dad. She was sure they must be dead for they would never have left them alone this long. Brittany knew she couldn't go looking for them because the little ones needed her and there was no way she would let Morgan go on his own; even if he thought he could do it, he was just too young. She thought about her Auntie Lana. She was coming out to be with them on the 23rd. Brittany had heard her mommy talking about it. She just had to hang on until Auntie came and then they would get help and try to find her parents. It was pretty clear that something bad had happened, either on the way to town or on their way back home. She was pretty sure though, that if her parents hadn't made it to town, her Auntie Lana would have sent somebody to check on them.

On the morning of December 17th, Brittany was up earlier than usual. All night she had tossed and turned and worried that the fire would go out. It was hard to get a fire going and she was always concerned that she would sleep too deeply and everyone would be frozen to death when she woke up.

She quietly pulled on her clothes so she wouldn't waken anyone. She let everyone sleep while she packed the water to the thirsty animals in the barn. Once she had the animals fed and watered, her plan was to come back in and make breakfast for the little ones. Then she'd go out and milk the cow.

It was still dark outside. The blizzard had finally played itself out, but Brittany noticed that it was very cold as the snow crunched beneath her feet. It was on mornings like this that Brittany wished she had a dog. When Daddy came home she was going to tell him she wanted one. She wanted a great big dog, one that could protect her from mountain lions.

She set her pails of water on the ground and pulled open the barn door. Once inside, she found the lantern and lit it. The illumination made eerie shadows on the wall. The cow gave a moo of greeting and the calf in the other pen darted to her feet. Eager to eat, the calf started bawling and woke the pigs and chickens. The calf knew that once Brittany had taken enough milk from his mother for the family's needs he would be turned loose to enjoy the milk remaining in the udder. Pouring water into the troughs, Brittany laughed at the calf, "You're going to have to drink a little water and eat some grain for awhile because it's too early to milk. You won't starve, don't worry."

Brittany picked up the heavy wooden buckets and went back to the house to get the other two pails of water. After this she'd be done with the water hauling. By the time she made her return trip it was about eight o'clock. She dumped the last pail of water into the pigs' trough and thought, "Oh, the heck with it, I might as well milk the cow and get it over with."

The calf, still bawling for its mother, helped to make up her mind. Once she had her share of the milk, she turned the calf loose. Butting at his mother's teat, the calf sucked greedily as if there was never going to be another meal for him. Brittany waited and watched until the greedy little fellow was finished and then put him back into his own pen. Turning the lantern off, Brittany pushed open the barn door and stepped outside into the cold morning once again.

As she started toward the cabin, Brittany heard something behind her in the semi-darkness. She turned and, as her eyes adjusted to the darkness, she saw a huge wolf baring its snarling teeth. Frightened tears ran down Brittany's face. Her heart was pounding so hard she thought the wolf could hear it. How could this be happening – a mountain lion one day and a wolf the next? And this time there was no Morgan to help her. Her legs were trembling so badly she didn't think she could move. The cabin was about 100 feet from her and the wolf about 50. What was she going to do? Suddenly, she made a decision and ran toward the cabin. The wolf was almost on top of her when she stopped short and swung the heavy milk pail, striking it across the side of its head. The sudden slap in the face stunned the wolf enough to give Brittany the seconds she needed to run through the door that, miraculously, Morgan was holding open. Slamming the door in the wolf's face as he lunged at the opening gave Brittany a sadistic pleasure. She hoped she'd broken his nose.

The screaming and hollering had woken and frightened the little girls. Brittany was trying to hush them when the wolf hit the door again. Morgan ran to get the bar that fit across the inside of the door and shoved it into place. Brittany sat a crying Ashley on the bed and ran to push the shutters closed as well. If the wolf could almost knock a big log door down, there was no reason that he couldn't fly through a pane of glass and get at them. Getting the gun, Morgan shot a bullet through the door the next time the wolf hit it. Finally, all was quiet. Everyone in the cabin was subdued. No one was even praising Morgan for chasing the wolf away. Worst of all, the young boy wasn't feeling very brave at all. He didn't want this full-time job of killing bad animals – he just wanted his mom.

As Brittany prepared breakfast, she was very glad that she had done the chores early and that she had milked the cow when she did. There was absolutely no way that she would go to the barn now with the possibility that the wolf might still be out there. She was awful happy that the barn door had to be pulled open rather than pushed because if the wolf was trying to get in, he couldn't. The next time she needed to go out for water, snow, or chores Morgan was coming with her and bringing the gun. The little girls, scared or not, would have to stay inside and watch for them through the windows. If they had been out with her this morning, there was no way she could have protected them. She shuddered at the thought as she put hot oatmeal on the table for breakfast.

"Morgan," she said, "We're going outside right now to chop wood and bring in snow. The wolf is probably gone for now, but you are going to stand right there with the gun while I chop a bunch. We are going to bring in enough wood to last two or three days. We'll bring in extra snow and fill whatever extra pots we have. Getting the snow in isn't as bad as the wood chopping because it doesn't take so much time. From now on I'm only going to water the animals and milk the cow once a day. I will go out around four o'clock and lock up the calf and only milk the cow in the mornings. Then I'll let him out with his mother until the next day at four o'clock. That way she won't be too swollen with milk and we will have enough milk. We won't be going outside any more than we have to because where there's one wolf, I'm sure there are two or more."

So Brittany chopped and carried in wood and snow while Morgan stood guard with the rifle. They didn't quit until Brittany was satisfied that there was enough. Morgan was pretty well frozen from standing in one spot, but the boy didn't complain. If something happened to his sister, there was no way he could even split the wood, let alone cook and look after the little girls by himself.

Once they were back in the house, Brittany was pleased to see that the little girls had made the beds, washed the breakfast dishes, and swept the floor. It being well past noon, she made some soup and toast and then said, "Come, kids, let's all lie down for a rest. I'll read you some stories, then we'll get up, and maybe we'll play some games of marbles."

Relaxing, Brittany looked at the children lying all around her. They had all fallen asleep. Brittany, who hadn't slept all night, closed her eyes to rest them, thinking about the mountain lion and the wolf ordeal until she fell into a deep sleep.

Later, Ashley woke up and sat up looking at everyone sleeping around her. Lying down again, she put her little hands to Brittany's face and patted her cheek. She loved her big cousin so much and she didn't like it when Brittany cried or was feeling sad. She cuddled closer to Brittany, kissed her cheek, and said, "Me help you, Bitty. Me help Bitty." The little girl snuggled her "tutu blue," which was her blanket. Why she called it a tutu blue no one seemed to know. It had blue lining, but how she got tutu blue out of the word blanket puzzled everyone. When she misplaced or couldn't find the blanket she went around calling for it. If she really couldn't find it and needed everyone's help, she would holler at the top of her voice, "Tutu blue, where you are?"

The little girl was the apple of everyone's eye. Brittany, Morgan, and Sydnee doted on her. The only one that bucked Ashley was Rachel, who didn't hesitate to clobber the spoilt little girl once in awhile. Managing to climb to the floor without waking anyone, Ashley pulled her coat from its hook and put it on. Doing the buttons up crookedly, she pushed her little feet into her boots not realizing they were on the wrong feet. Finding her toque and little mitts, she said out loud, "Dress warm, me warm. Me get wood. Me help Bitty, Bitty no cry no more."

Poor little baby thought the reason Brittany cried was because she hated to chop wood. Getting a chair, she pushed it over to the door, crawled up on it, and lifted the latch. "Me tough," she said as she lifted the latch with both hands. Once the latch was up she crawled down and pushed the chair back to the table. Going back to the door, she stopped to pick up her tutu blue, pulled the door open, and went outside. She wrapped her tutu blue around her neck and went to the woodpile. She found a piece of wood she could carry and took it back inside the cabin and hollered, "Me help, Bitty!" But no one stirred in the bed. She went back outside and she could hear the calf bawling in the barn. "Me go feed calf," she said and headed towards the barn.

The cold seeping into the cabin from the open door woke Brittany. Flying from the bed, she shoved the door closed. She looked around wondering how the door had come open. The wolf could have come in and killed them. Looking at the bed, Brittany thought she was going to faint as the blood rushed to her head.

"The baby, oh my God, the baby is gone!" she screamed. "Morgan, Ashley's gone!" Her eyes flying to the coats and boots, she noticed that the baby's were missing. She ran to the cupboard and grabbed the big butcher knife. Pushing her feet into her boots, she ran out the door screaming Ashley's name, "Ashley! Where are you?"

By this time, Morgan and the little girls were awake. "Watch Rachel," Morgan said to Sydnee, "Ashley's gone."

Morgan panicked, wondering why Brittany hadn't taken the gun. Hurriedly, he put on his coat and boots, grabbed the rifle, and told the crying little girls, "You stay inside 'til someone comes for you. Keep the door closed. I have to go help Brittany."

Running as fast as he could, Morgan raced over to the barn to help. Brittany screamed out Ashley's name. The little girl didn't answer. Holding the big butcher knife high, Brittany ran towards the barn and then stopped dead in her tracks. The big wolf was standing in front of Ashley, who was backed up against the side of the barn. Brittany could hear her crying and saying, "Go away you bad puppy. No bite Ashee." Tears were running down her little cheeks and blood dripped from her little hand. The wolf had no pity for the little girl and continued to snarl and snap at her.

Brittany knew she had no time left. She raised the knife as she ran towards the wolf, screaming at it to leave the baby alone. Somebody was going to die and it wasn't going to be her little Ashley. "Run, Ashley! Go to the cabin," Brittany screamed at the baby.

The wolf turned on Brittany. She watched everything in slow motion as the wolf ran at her and Ashley ran toward the cabin, pulling her tutu blue behind her. Any other time it would have been hilarious to see the baby not forget her tutu blue, which she thought could protect her from anything.

Suddenly, a large man with shoulder-length golden hair stood between Brittany and the wolf. Brittany blinked. It seemed as if he had dropped out of the sky right in front of her. He reached out for the wolf that had launched at Brittany. Catching the wolf with both hands, he tossed the animal aside as if it weighed nothing at all. Landing on its back, the wolf lay stunned. The man walked over to the wolf as it regained its feet and lunged again. The man simply reached out and slapped it sharply alongside the jaw. The wolf stood, swaying, as the man said, "Get home where you belong. What are you doing attacking a baby? Shame on you! I'll talk to you later." With his huge head down and tail tucked between his legs, the wolf turned and ran toward the trees.

By this time Morgan, holding the rifle, was crouched beside his sister, who had collapsed in terror. The little girls were coming from the cabin with Sydnee carrying a crying Ashley and her tutu blue. "Come help me!" she cried out, "The baby's bleeding really bad."

Rachel, who was totally white in the face, looked at the wolf running away, the blood, and Brittany, and then fainted dead away. Morgan ran to Rachel and, setting his rifle down in the snow, picked her up in his scrawny little arms. He was stronger than he looked. Lugging Rachel back to the cabin, he hollered at Sydnee, "Bring the baby back to the cabin. I told you not to come outside and when I tell you something you listen to me! What if the wolf wasn't dead and if the man hadn't come or if I went to shoot him and missed? He would kill all of you!" Unshed tears shone from his eyes as he reached the cabin and gently placed Rachel on the bed.

Walking over to Brittany, Gabriel gathered the crying young girl into his arms as if she weighed nothing and said, "My name is Gabriel. Do not be afraid. I am here to help you." Striding to the cabin, Gabriel could hear the baby crying. Sydnee met him at the door with tears running down her face. He laid the weeping Brittany on the bed as Rachel began to stir. He glanced over at the slender boy whose eyes were shining as he held back his tears. Pity filled Gabriel's heart. The little boy was trying so hard to be the man of the house and to be brave and, of course, men don't cry. Gabriel went to him first and said, "It's okay to cry. Brave men cry and they're fools if they don't."

Weeping, the sobs burst out of the little boy in a gush as he threw himself into Gabriel's arms saying, "I want my mom!"

Hugging him Gabriel said, "I've gone and done things badly. I've got all your women folk crying. I'll need some help, but first you'd better run outside and get your rifle out of the snow."

Taking Ashley from Sydnee's arms, Gabriel said, "We will tend to the baby first. I'll need some clean water, a needle, thread, and some bandages." Looking at the bitten hand he said to the baby, "What did that bad puppy do to you?"

"Puppy bite Ashee. He bad dog! See finga … owie."

Gabriel handed Ashley to Brittany and said, "You need to hold her real tight for me, Brittany. I have to put a few stitches in her hand where the bite is deep."

Brittany sat down on the chair and waited, comforting the baby, while everyone helped to get things ready for the little operation. Rachel, who was up and around by this time, came running over to the table with the scissors. Gabriel said, "Rachel! Don't run with scissors in your hand."

"How do you know our names? Do you know us?" wondered Rachel.

"Oh, yes," said Gabriel. "I know you all quite well — I'm your guardian angel."

"You are?" the children asked excitedly, not really believing him.

"Oh, yes, I truly am! You have been having a really bad time but were doing exceptionally well until the wolf came. Then I had to step in to help you. Morgan, you did a good job of shooting that mountain lion yesterday, and Brittany you were unbelievably brave going to fight a huge wolf with just a knife. Sydnee and Rachel, you have been very helpful in looking after your little sister and helping Brittany and Morgan with all the chores. In fact, today is December 17th and I am going to stay with you now and help you 'til after Christmas. You are all pretty tired and worn out. Now let's help the baby here and get her little hand mended."

"Okay. Brittany, hold her really tight and you other kids make faces at her. Try to keep her attention away from me and what I'll be doing to her hand." As Gabriel started to stitch the little girl's hand, she screamed bloody murder and instead of trying to keep her mind off the stitching, the kids all joined in crying with her.

"Oh, poor baby!" Rachel cried, kissing the baby on the cheek.

"It's okay, baby, it's okay, you'll be all right," Sydnee sobbed, patting her on the head.

Morgan, handing Gabriel the scissors and bandages, hiccoughed on a sob, and Brittany cried soundlessly as tears ran down her cheeks. Ashley, loving all the attention, cried, "Me alwight, me alwight. No cry. Ashee okay." Gabriel finished and put a clean bandage on the little girl's hand and then leaned over and kissed it. "Me okay. You good boy." Then she started to cry, "Dumb-dumb hurt owie."

Holding the crying baby, Brittany went to the bed and lay down with her, cuddling her in her arms to put her to sleep. Within ten minutes the oldest and the youngest were sound asleep, played out from their horrendous ordeal. Gabriel covered them with a heavy quilt and whispered to the other children, "Bundle up good. We're going outside to do the chores and play a few games while they rest."

Darkness had fallen by the time they had finished doing the chores and playing. It seemed like such a long time since they had been able to relax and just be children. The rosy-faced children were happy to have an adult around. Everything had changed. The fear of being alone quickly lifted and they all enjoyed their guardian angel. He was a lot of fun.

Gabriel made supper and told the children some wonderful stories about Heaven, Christmas, and the birth of Baby Jesus. By nine o'clock they were all were tucked into their beds, sound asleep, and Gabriel had settled in front of the fire.

He smiled to himself knowing the children didn't really believe that he was their guardian angel. The children weren't the only ones who were going to have the challenge of believing in something they had never seen. Actually, children have greater faith than adults. This Christmas was one these children would never forget and this story would be handed down for generations to come.

Around two o'clock in the morning, Brittany sleepily staggered from her bed. "What are you doing, honey?" Gabriel asked.

"Oh, I woke to put more wood on the fire so it won't go out."

"Go back to bed," Gabriel said, "I, Gabriel, am here to look after you and the fire, Brittany."

The little girl crawled back into bed and Gabriel heard her say, "Thank you God for sending your angel. We sure do need him."

On the morning of the 18th at breakfast, Gabriel said to the children, "After the morning chores, let's go find a Christmas tree. Tonight we can make decorations for it and if it's not too late, we will decorate it. Find a billycan to make hot chocolate and we'll take some sandwiches. Also, let's take some of those canned sausages your mother has in the cellar, the meat she was saving for a rainy day. The children all giggled. How could he know that's what their mother said about the special sausages she made only once a year for Christmas?

They all bundled up warmly for their tree-hunting expedition. The weather was still very cold and Gabriel said he didn't want anyone getting frostbite on their toes and feet. Gabriel carried the lunch and axe. The children romped and rolled in the snow having a merry time. Helping one another over snowdrifts and fallen logs, they giggled at one another as they frolicked in the deep snow. Gabriel smiled to himself as he watched the children enjoying themselves. It was good to see them free of worry.

However, it wasn't long before Ashley was tired and demanding to be carried, "Me hurt. Me carry axe. Bad boy carry Ashley?"

Gabriel laughed out loud as he handed Morgan the axe. He scooped her up into his arms and put her up around his neck. Ashley said, "Ashee scared dumb-dumb."

He asked the other children where she had picked up the words "bad boy" and "dumb-dumb." They all shook their heads and shrugged their shoulders.

Rachel said, "We don't know and I'm tired of telling her it's not nice to call people those names. When she's mad at Morgan she calls him 'bad boy'. I guess she's mad at you for hurting her owie."

Gabriel exclaimed, "Of course that's why she's mad at me!"

It didn't take long for them to find a tree to their liking. Gabriel chopped it down, and then after a brief search they found a little clearing for their picnic. Gabriel made a fire, melted snow in the billycan, and then added chocolate, milk, and sugar from a jar that they had mixed and brought from home. He cut sticks and whittled the ends to a point. Opening the jar of sausages, he skewered a sausage on the end of each stick to heat over the fire. Munching their lunch of peanut butter sandwiches, sausages, and hot chocolate, the children agreed they had never tasted anything so good. Gabriel told them this was because food always tasted best eaten outside after a hard tromp in the fresh air.

They relaxed around the fire, enjoying the warmth it radiated. Chilled hands and toes were soon toasty warm as they sat leaning against one another. Gabriel told them more stories about heaven and what God expected from the people on earth. As he talked, he reached down to put more wood on the fire. Ashley jumped up and said, "Me help bad boy," as she tried to pick up a piece of wood that was much too big for her.

Gabriel grabbed her and said, "No – me help you – before you fall into the fire." Laughing, he said to the children, "I'm never going to get on her good side, am I?" The little girl just glared at him.

Gabriel heard Brittany gasp, "The wolf is back!"

Gabriel stood up. Sure enough, there was the huge wolf that had terrorized the little family the day before. "Come here, wolf," Gabriel said. The wolf timidly approached Gabriel with its head and tail down. The children all hid behind Gabriel in a tight circle, peeking out at the wolf. Brittany held Ashley tightly in her arms. In terror they watched the wolf as Gabriel reached out to pet him. They heard him say, "I'm sorry I had to hurt you. You weren't supposed to hurt these children and scare them like you did. I want you to show these children that you're sorry for what you did to them. You scared them very badly."

Gabriel stood aside so the wolf could approach the children. Reaching out slowly, the wolf gently licked Ashley's face. He stood quietly as Morgan, Sydnee, and Rachel shyly and tentatively pet him. He was so peaceful the children couldn't believe that this was the same beast that had tried so hard to kill them. The children fed the wolf some of the leftover peanut butter sandwiches and sausages. Everyone held their breath as Ashley, holding a piece of meat, had to push things a little further by putting her little hand right into the wolf's mouth. The wolf gently took the meat, swallowed it in one gulp, and then proceeded to wash Ashley's face with his long tongue. Soon the wolf and children were rolling around and chasing each other through the snow.

The only one who wouldn't join in was Brittany. She wasn't about to forgive the animal for trying to hurt her and the baby. She didn't trust him. The wolf, sensing her dislike and distrust, came slowly up to her wagging his tail. Sitting down in front of her, he gave a pitiful whine as if saying he was sorry. The other children watched in wonder as forgiveness filled Brittany's heart and she reached out gingerly to pet him. The wolf stood and edged in closer to the young girl so she could put her arms around his neck and hug him.

Gabriel spoke, "It's a good thing you did, Brittany – to forgive him – because I think you would have been stuck with him until you did."

Suddenly, there was the call of another wolf from the heavy forest. The wolf, which was still in Brittany's arms, threw his head back and gave a howl in return. Then he looked at Gabriel as if to ask if it was okay for him to go. Gabriel nodded and the wolf, with one long look back at the children as if to remember them, disappeared into the trees.

The children all stood there with open mouths watching the wolf go. They were intrigued that the wolf had been so nice to them and to the big man. Sydnee said, "You really must be an angel to make that wolf be nice."

Gabriel nodded his head, "I told you, I am an angel."

At home they eagerly did the evening chores, first helping Gabriel outside with Brittany and Sydnee inside making supper. They hurried through supper, anxious to get started on the decorations for the Christmas tree. While making popcorn, they used food colouring to make different colours. Then, with a needle and thread they made long strings of coloured popcorn to wrap around the tree. Next, they took acorns, coloured them different colours, put string through the tips, and hung them on the tree. The little girls drew bells, balls, and angels on paper and cut them out to be hung on the tree.

Gabriel was busy making an angel out of rags wrapped around a piece of wood. Taking some bark off the wood, he made wings. Then he used yellow wool to fashion hair and glued it to the top of the angel's head. Then, taking some food colouring, he gave her blue eyes and red lips and placed her on top of the tree. The little ones clapped their hands joyfully and stood back to admire their beautiful Christmas tree.

They eventually got into their pyjamas and nestled down with blankets on the floor in front of the fireplace to listen again to Gabriel's stories. With only the light from the fireplace the angel on top of the tree took on a radiant light of its own. The silent children could not take their eyes off the beauty of that radiant angel, each one thinking it was the firelight that was making her shine.

But later that night, Gabriel heard Brittany crying softly, trying not to waken the sleeping children. Gabriel left his chair in front of the fire and went over to her. "What's the matter, Brittany? Why are you crying?" he asked.

"Oh, Gabriel, I think my Mommy and Daddy are dead. They would never go and leave us this long by ourselves. I must try to go to town if my Auntie Lana doesn't come. She is supposed to be here on the 23rd and spend Christmas with us. Tomorrow will be the 20th and I want my Auntie to come. I don't even know if Mommy and Daddy made it to town. Maybe Auntie Lana is wondering where they are too. Maybe she thinks that they just decided not to go into town this year because it is so cold. I don't know what to think!" She began to cry harder. "Maybe the wolves or a lion ate them."

Gabriel lifted the little girl into his arms and said, "I think they're okay, honey. Don't forget that they have guardian angels to watch over them as well. I'll tell you what though, if no one comes in the next couple of days, I will go and look for them."

"Oh, would you, Gabriel? I would be so happy if you would."

Placing her back on the bed, Gabriel said, "Say your prayers, Brittany, and believe in what you pray for. Then go to sleep. Everything will work out if you just believe."

For the first time since her parents left, Brittany fell into a well-deserved sleep, but not until after she had talked to her Lord. And she thanked him profusely for sending them one of his angels.

❅   ❅   ❅

By six the next morning, Joseph had the horse and sleigh waiting by the back door of Lana's shop. The air was so bitterly cold it took his breath away. As Lana helped him pack the sleigh with Christmas presents and food, Joseph laughed and said, "I feel like St. Nicholas!" He had been doing his best to take her mind off the family she was missing and worrying about, but he hadn't been too successful. They were supposed to leave on the 23rd, but the young woman couldn't wait any longer. They were leaving today, the 20th of December.

Joseph had finished rebuilding her home and it was beautiful, even if he had to say so himself. Beds and furniture had been moved in and set into place. The table with its beautiful doily was awaiting its first meal. Two large easy chairs, and three little chairs made in the same fashion as the large ones, sat in front of the fireplace awaiting the presence of the three little girls they had been made for.

As they rode along, Lana noticed a cross on the donkey's back. She said, "Gee, Joseph, I've never noticed that your donkey has a cross pattern in his fur."

Joseph looked at her and smiled and said, "All donkeys have the cross on their backs."

"Really? That's unusual. I have never noticed it before, but then I haven't been around that many donkeys."

Joseph said, "The cross is a sign from God. Mary, the mother of Jesus, rode a donkey to Bethlehem where He was born and Jesus rode on a donkey into Jerusalem to be crucified. God paid homage to the ass, a lowly creature, for carrying the Christ to his birth and to his death."

"What a lovely story," Lana said.

"It's not a story, Lana," Joseph said quietly. "It's the truth."

Snow crunched beneath the horse and sleigh as they rode along in thoughtful silence until Joseph said, "I have a friend whose name is Nick. He lives about fifteen miles from town. I was just wondering if maybe we could stop there for breakfast and say hello. What do you think? It would give us time to warm up and rest the horse and my old donkey. Then the rest of the trip won't feel so long. We won't stay too long."

"Okay," Lana said, "I won't mind having a rest and a hot breakfast. I could use one and it will be nice to eat someone else's cooking for a change. Have you known this Nick very long? I thought you were new to these parts."

Joseph smiled and said, "Nick and I have been friends for many years. I stop in whenever I'm needed."

"Needed?" Lana exclaimed, "Were you needed by Nick, Joseph? You should have said so! You could have taken a few days off from building to visit him."

"Oh, this is soon enough. I'm sure Nick has everything under control by now."

They reached Nick's place by ten. The deep snow made it slow going at times, but, all in all, the horse wasn't having too much difficulty pulling the sleigh. When they arrived Lana was surprised and said, "I have been out to Darren's a few times and have never noticed this house here before. It's so quaint with its cottage style roof and four gables – I love it! It's funny that Darren never pointed it out to me before either, surely he knows it's here."

As Joseph was helping Lana down from the sleigh, she said, "Just wait a minute, Joseph. I have some cookies I want to take in for Nick and his family." She found the cookies and turned around in time to see a handsome old man with white hair and a beard to match greeting Joseph with a hug on the front porch.

"Joseph! Hello, my old friend. How are you?"

The two elderly gentlemen hugged and greeted one another heartily, and then Joseph introduced Lana to Nick. Holding her hand, Nick said, "My, Lana, you've grown into a fine young lady."

"You know me?" Lana asked. "I'm sorry, I don't remember you."

Nick, taking in the beauty of the slender blonde, blue-eyed young woman, said, "Oh, yes, my dear, we met years ago when you were just a child, a child with a wonderful imagination."

"Oh," Lana replied feeling very confused. Something in her long-forgotten memory made this charming old man seem familiar, but she didn't know what it was.

"Come in … come in and warm yourselves by the fireplace. I will call Ava and she will get you something hot to drink and fix something to eat." Nick hurried from the room to call his wife and soon they were back with hot chocolate and toast.

As they ate, Nick said, "A couple of weeks back I came upon a bad accident. I found a young couple who were badly hurt and brought them here. If I hadn't found them when I did, they would have died from the cold. They were in very grim condition. I would like you to meet them. Maybe you know them or have seen them in town."

Lana's heart pounded in her chest and she asked, "Was the man a big man and the woman a tiny woman?"

"Why, yes," said Nick.

"Were there five children with them?" Lana asked, the words barely coming out in a whisper.

"No," Nick answered, "There were no children with them."

It couldn't be Darren and Alison, thought Lana, for they would have had the children with them.

"Well, come and meet them. Maybe you can help me find out who they are." Joseph and Lana followed Nick up the stairway of the beautiful home. White starched doilies lay on the quaint old furniture adding lustre to the dark mahogany. The walls were hung with beautiful pictures of winter scenes. The windows were adorned in sparkling white curtains. It was so homey one wished that one could stay forever in the peace that seemed to reign over the household.

As they walked down the corridor to a bedroom, Nick informed them that, in just the last few days, he had started to communicate with the patients. "The only thing they have been saying is, 'the kids, the kids'. But they haven't been staying awake long enough for me to figure out who the kids are. The woman is in worse shape than the man. She took a terrible blow to the head. I had to remove some fingers from the man's hands because they were so badly frozen. I believe he froze them while trying to make a shelter. He did a good job though, if he hadn't, they would never have survived."

As they walked into the room, Lana said, "Darren ... Alison ..." and fainted dead away. Joseph caught her in his arms before she fell to the floor. He carried her to a sofa near another fireplace and laid her gently on it. When she came around Lana was shocked at the sight of the couple. Their faces were red and chapped. Frozen skin had peeled from their faces, leaving them looking as if they had a bad case of sunburn. Rising up off the sofa, Lana went to her brother's side and, taking his hand in hers, she said, "What happened, Darren? Where are the kids?"

Speaking weakly, voice trembling, Darren managed to get out what had happened. They had left the kids alone at the cabin, and they had been gone since December 2nd. Finally, he could speak to someone who knew about the existence of the kids, "I've been so afraid, but I couldn't talk or come around long enough to explain the situation."

Nick, feeling Lana's panic along with her brother's, said, "Today's the 20th. You and Joseph should carry on to the cabin. These two need a few more days to recuperate. I'll take them to their home on Christmas Day. You go on ahead, and if anything is wrong Joseph can come back for me. I have a feeling that your family is all right. Gabriel is probably there by now looking after them."

"Gabriel?" Lana asked, "Who is Gabriel?"

"Their guardian angel," Nick replied.

Lana, thoroughly confused, exclaimed, "That's not very funny and this is no time for jokes or fairy tales."

Nick never blinked an eye and said, "It's not a joke. Gabriel is their guardian angel."

Lana still confused and concerned said, "Darren, how come you left the kids alone rather than bringing them with you?"

Darren weakly explained that, since they weren't going to be gone longer than three days, they thought the children would be okay. The weather had been between 40 and 50 degrees below zero and the kids wanted to stay home where it was warm. He explained how Brittany insisted that she could do the chores and look after the little ones for a couple of days.

Lana nodded her head. Of course, it's true that Brittany is capable of handling the children.

Alison, who had been sleeping when the group had entered the room, woke and spotted Lana. Crying, she said, "Lana, I have been waiting for you to find us for so long."

Lana hurried over to her weeping sister-in-law. Sitting on the edge of the bed, Lana comforted Alison, holding her in her arms. Alison said, "I'm so afraid for the children. We never should have left them by themselves. Oh, what have we done?"

Rocking Alison in her arms, Lana said, "We have pretty spunky kids and if anybody can keep them together, it's our Brittany."

Darren started to cry. "I'm so sorry, Lana, we shouldn't have left them alone. We should have taken them with us."

Detangling herself from Alison, she walked back over to her brother, reached down and hugged him. "Don't cry. From what you and Nick told me about the accident it's a wonder you and Alison are still alive. If the five children had been with you, the chances of them all surviving would probably have been pretty slim. I believe they're safe at home. I know they will be alive as long as Brittany can keep the fire going and feed them. If she can do that, they'll be fine until I get there."

Ava, who had been scurrying here and there trying to comfort the parents, said, "For land's sake! No wonder you poor youngsters couldn't get better – you were sick with worry for the children."

Lana, who was by now getting very concerned, said, "I'd like to get going now, Joseph, if we could."

Joseph nodded his head in agreement.

She walked over to Alison and said, "If anything is wrong, I will send Joseph back right away. Kissing and hugging her family farewell so soon after finding them made the tears fall harder.

Once Joseph and Lana had dressed themselves in their winter clothing, Nick and Ava walked them to the sleigh. Hugging Lana, Nick said, "Don't be frightened, child, your babies are safe."

Hugging Nick back, Lana said, "I hope so. I don't think I could live without my children. I know my poor sister-in-law feels the same way. She's beside herself with worry. I hope that God hears our prayers."

Nick patted her on the shoulder saying, "Oh, He does, Lana, He does."

After bundling them into the sleigh under the heavy warm hides, Nick watched the two travellers until they were out of sight. As he walked back to the house, fluffy snowflakes began to fall.

The next thirty miles went very slowly. Bucking the heavy snowdrifts, the horse grew tired. Lana and Joseph climbed off the sleigh several times to help the horse pull through the worst places. The heavy snowfall made it hard to see and Joseph, relying on Lana's directions, began to worry that they might get lost. The pack of howling wolves following them didn't help their state of mind, nor quell the nervousness of the horse and donkey.

It was eleven o'clock that night when they saw a flickering of light in the darkness. The tension of the wolves, the darkness, cold, and worry over the children finally overtook Lana and she began to cry.

As they drew up to the cabin, the door opened. Standing in the doorway was the biggest man Lana had ever seen. Not only the biggest she had ever seen, but also the most handsome. To top it off, this Hercules of a man had shoulder-length golden hair. He came out and grabbed the horse's reins saying, "Hello, Joseph. Hello, Lana. You finally got here. We have been waiting a long time for you. Joseph, you help Lana into the cabin and then you and I will unload the sleigh. We'd better hurry though. The wolves are on the prowl and the sooner we get this horse and donkey put away, the safer we'll be."

Lana leapt from the sleigh and ran to the house, eager to see her children. She was halted abruptly by the welcome sight of the five beautiful children she had been so worried about. Ashley, of course, was sleeping facing Brittany with her tutu blue wrapped around her neck and one bandaged little hand resting on her cousin's cheek. Morgan was sleeping in his little bed next to the little girls' big bed along the wall.

Lana sat down on the edge of the bed beside Rachel and Sydnee. Reaching out, she caressed their soft little faces. Never had she been so thankful for anything in her life. Falling on her knees, she lowered her head and thanked God for the lives of the children. While she prayed she also thanked Him for saving Darren and Alison and for sending Nick, Joseph, and the huge man to whom she hadn't yet been introduced.

The men brought the presents and supplies into the cabin and Lana put everything away, hiding the presents under the beds so the children wouldn't discover them. When she was finished she sat down in a chair beside the fire and, overwhelmed by the beautiful Christmas tree, she basked in the luxury and warmth of the fire.

The men weren't long bedding the horses down and soon they entered the cabin, talking and laughing as if they were old friends. Lana was still confused about all this. Joseph, who wasn't from anywhere near here, seemed to know each and every one of them. Joseph introduced the big man as Gabriel. Lana took a step backwards and laughed and said, "Oh, you're the one Nick called the children's guardian angel. I'm so glad to meet you."

Gabriel and Joseph looked at each other as if sharing a secret and Gabriel said, "He did, did he?" He set about preparing tea and buttered biscuits for everyone, then served Joseph and Lana in front of the roaring fireplace. Lana had so many questions to ask Gabriel, but she could hardly keep her eyes open. The heat of the fire warmed her cold body, the relief of finding all her loved ones safe calmed her mind, and now peace of mind and exhaustion were lulling Lana to sleep.

Gabriel, conscious of her physical state, said, "We have a lot to talk about, but it will keep for tomorrow when everyone's rested up."

Standing, Lana mumbled sleepily, "Thank you for the hot tea and biscuits. They were so tasty, just what I needed. You're right though, I'm so tired I can hardly stand up."

Finding her bag with her nightclothes, she dressed in Darren and Alison's bedroom then came out and said, "I will sleep with Brittany and Ashley. Joseph, you can share Darren's bed with Gabriel."

"I'll sleep in front of the fire on this long chair," Gabriel said. "I have a warm blanket and this way I can keep an eye on the fire. Joseph, go rest your old bones and have a good night's sleep." They bade one another goodnight and it wasn't long before the soft sounds of sleep filled the cabin.

Lana woke in the morning with little arms wrapped around her neck and Ashley kissing her face. Rachel, Sydnee, Morgan, and Brittany were jumping on the bed laughing and hollering in delight at the sight of their mother and auntie.

The noise woke Joseph and Gabriel. It was bedlam with all the excitement so Gabriel and Joseph took the opportunity to escape from the cabin to do the chores. By the time Lana had made breakfast and helped the younger ones dress, the men were finished doing the chores and everyone sat down to eat. As they ate breakfast, words tumbled out of the children, each of them trying to tell Lana everything that had happened. Lana noticed Brittany's unusually solemn face. It seemed that in just two months she had grown up. When the children got to the part of the story where Brittany had run to save the baby with only a butcher knife in her hand, Lana started to cry. Getting up she went around the table to Brittany, who fell into her aunt's arms saying, "Oh, Auntie, I was so scared!"

Lana, holding her tight, said, "Brittany, you have to be the bravest person I know. I don't even know if I could have been that brave."

With her arms still around the young girl she said, "I have some very good news for you and Morgan. Your Mom and Dad are okay. They had a really bad accident caused by a mountain lion, but a man named Nick found them and he's looking after them. He said he would bring them home on Christmas day." She went on to explain all that had happened up to the time Nick had found them. Brittany laid her head on her aunt's shoulder and cried, but this time they were tears of relief and joy.

Joseph said, "Let's all go outside and chop wood and haul in lots of snow because I think Auntie might want to wash clothes today."

"Yes," agreed Lana, "I want everything to be fresh for Christmas. Tomorrow I will start baking. We need fresh bread and goodies for treats."

"Good!" said Gabriel. "When we're finished the chores we'll take the children ice fishing. There's a fishing pond a couple of miles away. We'll catch a few fish for supper."

"That would be a nice change from canned moose meat and chicken," quipped Brittany.

Morgan piped up, saying, "Maybe I could take the rifle and hunt for a wild turkey for Christmas dinner while we're out there." Everybody happily agreed that a turkey would indeed make a wonderful meal on the most important day of the year. They had fresh chickens in the barn but turkey sure did sound delicious.

As soon as the men and children left, Lana got busy. She had a long day ahead of her. After washing the clothes and bedding, she hung everything outside to dry. Once they were out in the frozen air for a couple of hours, she brought everything in and hung the frozen articles by the fire to dry. By the time she had the beds remade and the washing done, she was pretty tired, but excited. She began to plan for something different for supper, something that would go with the fish they would catch.

Meanwhile, the little group headed for the frozen pond. Everyone was excited about going fishing. Gabriel and Joseph cut a couple of holes for the children. They placed the holes about a hundred feet apart so that there wouldn't be too much movement in one place, which would scare the fish away.

Brittany and Ashley shared one hole together and Sydnee and Rachel the other one. Joseph made a third hole for himself, cutting it extra big, hoping he could be the fisherman of the day by catching the biggest fish. Morgan and Gabriel headed into the buck brush to hunt for a turkey.

Joseph walked from hole to hole checking on the children. Everyone had caught a fish except Rachel. "Just be patient," Joseph said, when she remarked that everyone could catch fish except her. "You'll catch one too."

Joseph heard a shot, followed Gabriel and Morgan shouting at him to come and help them. The turkey had only been wounded and they would need Joseph to come and help them flush it out of the heavy brush. Warning the girls to be careful and not to get too close to the holes, he headed off to help Morgan and Gabriel.

Rachel, who was a having pangs of jealousy toward everyone because she was the only one without a fish, decided she would try Joseph's ice hole. Sydnee was antagonizing Rachel all the more by bragging about her own fishing skill. When Rachel headed toward the other hole, Sydnee started shouting at her to come back or she was going to be in big trouble. Rachel looked back at her big sister and hollered, "I don't have to listen to you!" And she walked right into the open hole.

The words, "Rachel, you smarten up," died on Sydnee's lips as she watched her sister disappear into the water. Running toward the hole where Rachel had disappeared, Sydnee screamed at Brittany to come. At the edge of the hole she fell to her tummy, still holding her fishing line in one hand, and slowly slid closer to the hole. Rachel's head popped back up through the hole. Sydnee reached out to grab her hand and looked into her little sister's terrified eyes.

"Sydnee, help me!" Rachel screamed.

The coldness of the water was already numbing her body. She tried to grasp the side of the ice, but her frozen little hands kept slipping off. Brittany had come up behind Sydnee and, hearing the crackling of the ice, she immediately got down on her belly. Grabbing Sydnee by the legs, Brittany screamed at her to grab Rachel's hand. Rachel went back under the water with only one little hand flailing above the surface. Sydnee gave a lurch, almost going in the water herself. Using every ounce of strength she had, she wrapped her fishing line around Rachel's wrist. She pulled as hard as she could and Rachel's head came up out of the water again. Sydnee screamed at her to hang on to the line with her other hand. Reaching out, Rachel grabbed the line wrapped around her other wrist. Hanging on to her little sister for dear life, Sydnee knew she wasn't strong enough to pull her from the water and that she needed help. If she couldn't hang on, Rachel would slip away under the ice and never be seen again.

Joseph and Gabriel had heard their screams and had come running. Seeing what was going on, Joseph said, "For Lord's sake, Gabriel! You're supposed to be looking after this sort of thing."

"I know, Joseph, but I got so excited about hunting that turkey I forgot everything else."

Gabriel quickly lay down on the ice and edged up beside Sydnee. He could hear the ice cracking around him and knew he had to hurry or they were all going to end up in the cold water. Taking the fishing line from Sydnee's tired little hands, he started to pull Rachel to him. When she was close enough that he could grab her hands, he hauled her out of the frigid water as fast as he could. Once Rachel was out he reached over and pushed Sydnee back toward Brittany, hollering at her to pull Sydnee back from the hole. Brittany pulled her cousin back to the edge of the pond before daring to stand up, afraid they would break through the cracking ice. Gabriel also stayed on his stomach, wiggling backward, pulling Rachel to safety.

Old Joseph grabbed the frozen little girl from Gabriel's arms and stripped her down to the skin. Getting her out of the already frozen clothes, he wrapped her in his big old raggedy but warm cloak. Holding her close to him, he tried to warm her with his own body. "Hurry, Gabriel, throw more wood on the fire. We have to get her warm." Thank goodness they had made a small fire when they had arrived to keep warm. Everyone helped gather the fish they had caught and bundled the fishing gear together while Joseph kept Rachel warm.

"Oh, my goodness. Morgan! Where is he?" Gabriel had forgotten all about him. What kind of guardian angel was he, forgetting about the little hunter? He started running toward the buck brush and then stopped for there was Morgan dragging the biggest turkey Gabriel had ever seen. Heaving a sigh of relief, Gabriel put his arm around the young boy's shoulders saying, "Good work, Morgan! We've had a bit of an accident and we have to hurry home. Come on, I'll tell you what has happened while we catch up to the others."

They hurried home with the cold little girl and a coatless Joseph. Gabriel said to Sydnee, "You sure are a brave little girl. You kids amaze me with your heroics. You saved your sister's life! If you hadn't tied that fishing line around your sister's hand, she would have gone under the ice."

Sydnee, trembling inside with fear, started sobbing. She had been so frightened for Rachel, and it had been all her fault. She had been bragging about how great she was at catching fish and making fun of her little sister. She would never, as long as she lived, forget the sound of the ice cracking beneath her. She had thought for sure that it was going to break and that she would disappear into that cold water along with Rachel.

Her thoughts went to her father – she missed him so much. She felt very sad inside and wished Daddy were with her right now to tell her that everything was going to be okay. Sydnee knew Mommy missed him too. He had been gone so long Sydnee didn't know if Rachel and Ashley could even remember him. Sometimes when she watched Brittany and Morgan with Uncle Darren she wanted to cry. It wasn't that Uncle Darren wasn't good to them, but it just wasn't the same as having her father.

Crying in earnest now, she thought of Grandpa Carson and Grandma Bev. She wished Grandma was here right now. Why did Grandpa have to break his leg and make it so they couldn't move here to be near them? She imagined her grandma's warm loving arms around her and cried even harder. Grandma would be scolding and loving her all at the same time if she had seen what just happened.

Gabriel finally picked up the heartbroken little girl. Cradling her in his arms, he said, "If you had one wish, Sydnee, what would you wish for?"

Through her tears Sydnee said, "I want my daddy to come home and my grandpa and grandma. I wish we could all be together for Christmas."

Gabriel nodded his golden head and said, "That's a wonderful wish. Who knows? More miracles happen at Christmas than at any other time of the year."

Joseph carried Rachel, Gabriel carried Sydnee, Brittany packed Ashley, and Morgan dragged his turkey back to the cabin. They arrived with all three little girls sound asleep. Exhausted, Brittany placed Ashley in her mother's arms and hurried back to her brother. The little guy was tired but so very proud of his huge Christmas turkey. As Brittany met him, he let her take one leg and between them they made the rest of the trip back to the cabin pulling the bird between them. When Brittany and Morgan finally got to the cabin Auntie had already dressed Rachel in warm pyjamas and tucked her into bed. Her mother had fed her some hot soup and it wasn't long until the little girl fell asleep with Sydnee lying beside her.

Sydnee woke crying, and told her mother how it was all her fault that Rachel had fallen into the lake. Lana shushed the crying child in her arms, consoling her until she too fell back to sleep, totally exhausted from her ordeal. That night, with her three little girls sleeping next to her, Lana thanked God again for His mercy and for sparing the lives of her little family. As sleep overtook her, her last thought was to wonder how in the world Brittany had managed to look after everything by herself. With only the other children to help her, she seemed to have managed better than the two grown men and herself. Ironically, Joseph and Gabriel were thinking the very same thing.

December 22nd dawned and the morning brought a Chinook wind. What a beautiful day it was. Lana kept Rachel in bed worrying that she might have caught a chill by being in the frozen water, but Rachel seemed no worse for wear. By dinnertime she was up and dressed, playing with the others.

Lana prepared a big batch of bread dough and made both loaves and buns. The smell of the fresh bread filled the cabin and made everyone's mouth water. She made a chicken stew to go with the fresh bread for the evening meal. It seemed she couldn't turn around without someone asking her if it was time to eat. As she put the supper on the table, the rest of the household sat close to the fireplace talking and relating stories about the cougar and the wolves. She listened as they described how Gabriel had come and saved them from the wolf.

Lana felt a bit irritated with Gabriel when he let the children go on exaggerating about how he had saved them from the wolf, and how when they went to get the tree the wolf had come again, and that he had let them pet it. It bothered her a little when he said he was their guardian angel. In a way he was, though, for he had helped them a lot. But he was going a little too far. After some time, and no longer able to contain herself, she said, "Gabriel, it's not right for you to let the children believe you're a real angel when you're not."

Gabriel gave Lana a beautiful smile and said, "Believe what you want, my dear, but don't take away the faith of the children and turn it into your own disbelief. They see and know something you won't accept."

Lana turned back to the stove, thinking to herself, "They see an angel and I don't."

As she set the supper on the table, she could hear Joseph telling them about stopping at Nick's. He described how well Darren and Alison were doing and how seriously they had been injured.

Morgan asked, "How is old Banjo? Is he okay?"

"No, Morgan," Joseph said, "He was killed when he went over the cliff, but thank heaven for that. Do you know why?"

Morgan shook his head sadly. "No. Why?"

"Well, because your dad needed Banjo's hide to help keep your mom and him warm. Your old horse, in his own way, saved their lives."

Morgan was glad old Banjo had helped save his parents, but still the little boy put his head down and cried for his old friend. Joseph hugged him, saying, "The best news is that Nick will be bringing your parents home on Christmas day! That will be the best present you've ever had, right?"

Lana called them to supper and as she said grace, she reached out and held Morgan's hand saying, "Please, Lord, look after Banjo and pet him once in awhile, maybe even take a ride on him. He was a very good horse."

On December 23rd Lana baked pies with everyone helping, some mixing the canned apples with flour and sugar while others rolled out piecrusts. They opened jars of pumpkin and blueberries and made three different kinds of pie. Then they sang Christmas carols and threw flour at one another, having a grand old time and forgetting for a while all the troubles they had come through. They howled with laughter when Gabriel took a blueberry spoon and touched Ashley on the nose with it. She told him in no uncertain terms what a bad boy and dumb-dumb he was. It seemed the more Lana checked her on the use of the frowned-upon word, the more it got used. Lana said, "Ashley, that's not a nice way to talk."

"Okay," she said, "Abril, you bad boy."

Around two o'clock in the afternoon Joseph said, "Let's all go sledding before we do chores."

And so they all dressed and went out for some fresh air. As she came down the hill on the sled with Ashley in front of her, Lana tried to remember the last time she'd had so much fun. It had been a long time since she had played with or had taken the time to just laugh with her girls.

That night after the children were in bed, Lana found some white wool in Alison's trunk. Out came the knitting needles. In moments her nimble hands flew as she started knitting a sweater for Gabriel. As Lana knit, it seemed the white wool took on a sparkly silver glow in the firelight. She held the wool closer to the light to see if her eyes were playing tricks on her. Lana thought her eyes must be tired and shrugged her shoulders. Tomorrow in the light it would just be white wool. Gabriel and Joseph had come in late so she had lots of time to knit in peace. They were spending a lot of time out in the shed after the children were in bed. Lana presumed they were making presents for the children for Christmas.

Finally, it was Christmas Eve. Lana couldn't wait for her brother and sister-in-law to come home. Her thoughts turned to her husband and she wondered where he was. Was he even alive? She didn't know. She hadn't heard from him in a very long time. Things hadn't been right between them when he left. He loved his little girls, though, and Lana thought that he must miss them terribly. Maybe someday he would come home.

Lana's mind turned back to the presents under the bed. Pulling them out, she placed them under the tree. She hoped Joseph would like his new cloak. Gabriel's sweater was something she couldn't get over. It was absolutely beautiful as was the scarf she had knit. Lana knew she had never made anything so lovely in her whole life.

When Lana was done she changed into her nightgown and sat by the fire looking at the Christmas tree. She couldn't remember a tree so lovely with its full body of branches. The children had done such a good job of decorating it. Earlier in the evening they had all sat around it singing carols. It had been a beautiful evening and now with the children all softly sleeping and the presents under the tree, it was truly peaceful in the little cabin.

The Three Saints of Christmas

Joseph and Gabriel still hadn't come inside so Lana crawled into bed and fell asleep. She dreamt that Gabriel was standing by the Christmas tree. He was handsome with his outstretched gleaming white angel wings that sprouted from his back. Beside him stood Joseph clothed in a beautiful blue robe. He had a halo glowing over the top of his head. Nick, all dressed in a red suit, was placing presents beneath the Christmas tree; in fact, he looked just like Santa Claus. They were laughing and talking to each other and sharing what looked like a drink of rum together. Lana had seen a bottle of rum in the cupboard and it seemed only fitting that the three old friends were sharing a drink. By golly, it was rum, with hot water and honey. A hot toddy – that's what her father used to call it. It was a comforting dream and Lana didn't even try to waken from it. She just slept on and waited for Christmas morning. In fact, when she woke in the morning the fantastic dream almost seemed real.

Back at Nick's cottage on Christmas Eve, Darren and Alison were allowed up and were helped out to a huge dining room where the loveliest meal they had ever seen was laid out on long tables. Nick, Ava, and their large family were all gathered around and clapped when the young couple was escorted into the room. Darren and Alison were surprised at the size of Nick and Ava's family, having only met the few that helped them from time to time. What surprised them most was that Nick's family members were very small people and the children were extra small in stature. Trying not to stare at the little people and trying to make them feel comfortable by telling them how lovely they all looked, Darren and Alison sat down at the table. Indeed, it was a beautiful sight.

The women were all attired in green evening gowns of every description. The men wore red suits and the children were all dressed in white, boys and girls alike. On the whole, they were all very attractive people and Nick had every right to be proud of his family.

Nick announced, "We are eating supper early as I have to make a few house calls tonight." Darren and Alison looked at each other. House calls? How could that be when they were the only ones who lived out this way? Of course, they could be wrong – after all they hadn't even known that Nick lived here. How they could have missed this place they didn't know.

"Alison and I had hoped that we could be home with our family tonight," said Darren.

Nick nodded his head saying, "Darren, I was going to try to get you home today, but Alison was feeling dizzy again so I thought it would be best for her to rest one more night. Alison turned her head, trying to hide the tears that fell to her cheeks. "Don't cry, dearie," Nick said. "Your children are fine or else Joseph would have come back. I know you're both disappointed, but the weather is terrible. It's at least 50 below zero. It's supposed to be warmer tomorrow. I don't want to risk your health; it's bad enough as it is. I have these deadlines to meet for tonight and we have been extremely busy, but I promise you I'll be back early and first thing in the morning I will be taking you home."

"Thank you, Nick," Alison said. "It's not that we want to sound ungrateful, it's just that we have been worried for so long about the children."

"I know, my dear, but I'm sure Gabriel was with the children long before Joseph and Lana arrived."

Darren gave Nick a puzzled look and asked, "Who is Gabriel?"

"Their guardian angel," replied Nick.

The young couple laughed. Well, Joseph had turned up for Lana, Nick had turned up for them, so why not Gabriel for the children? Nick acted as if the three men were all good friends and that each one was somewhere he was supposed to be. Maybe, when they were delirious they had been muttering about the children, and Nick had told his friend to go find the children. When Darren tried to ask Nick how he knew where to send this Gabriel, Nick changed the subject and began talking about his reindeer getting into some trouble with the children.

"I swear I'm in a dream at times," Darren said. "I feel as if we're part of some sort of miracle being played out."

Alison nodded her head in agreement, "I feel that way too. I can't believe that we're alive or that you found us in the deep snow or that we're going to go home tomorrow."

Nick looked at them, "Every day of life is a miracle and yes, you are part of a miracle. Because you have earned God's grace through your goodness and kindness to others you are to be reunited with your family."

"I don't know that we deserve all this praise," Darren said, "But thank you for bestowing it on us."

After supper Nick bade them goodnight and went off to do his errands while the rest of the family stayed around singing Christmas carols and visiting. Alison enjoyed playing with the little ones and visiting with the mothers. It had been a long time since she had enjoyed feminine company. As the children begin to get tired, the families began to leave for home. Darren and Alison bade them all goodnight and goodbye in case they didn't get to see them before they left in the morning. Thanking them for the lovely evening and all their help in the last two weeks, they invited them to stop in for a visit if they were ever in their area.

When everyone had left they said goodnight to Ava, who was sitting peacefully by the fire. As Alison was leaving the room, she said to Ava, "I'm so sorry that Nick had to go out tonight, especially with it being Christmas Eve."

Ava looked at her and said with a smile, "Oh, I'm used to it. He's being doing it for at least a couple of thousand years!"

Darren and Alison laughed at her joke and Alison said, "I know how you feel, I feel that way too, when Darren's gone."

As they limped to bed helping each other, Darren said, "You know it's amazing how weak I still feel. I hope I get feeling better pretty soon."

"I know," Alison said. "It seems as if it's been forever since we left our kids. I find myself crying a lot. At first I thought it was because I didn't feel well, but I think I have a really bad case of homesickness. Thank God Lana came early and is with the kids; I feel so much better knowing she's with them. That old man was a kind and gentle soul. I'll bet the kids love having him around."

They got ready for bed and blew out the lamp. The light of the moon entered the window illuminating everything in the room. Looking out at the cold clear night, they tried to remember when they had seen anything so beautiful as the white glistening snow in the moonlight. As they stood silhouetted in the window holding hands, they bowed their heads and thanked God for their lives and for the safety of their children.

❄ ❄ ❄

Three days before Christmas, early in the morning, Carson and Bev, along with Brodie, left Peace River for the 60-mile trip to North Star. There hadn't been a break in the cold weather for weeks so they were overjoyed to find the morning had brought the warm Chinook wind. Brodie had helped Carson load the sleigh the night before and had come over early in the morning to help harness the team of horses. Brodie was the same age as Morgan but a bit larger in size. Carson was grateful for his help as he stumbled around on his bum leg. Once the horses were ready they settled themselves in the sleigh, happy they had made the decision and glad to be on their way.

Bev was tired though. She had nearly killed herself getting everything ready: buying and wrapping presents, baking long into the evenings, and scurrying around preparing for the trip. Carson, trying to help, only ended up annoying her and getting in her way. Now, with the sound of the sleigh in the snow filling her ears, she smiled to herself, happy with her choices of gifts for the children. The looks on their faces when they opened their gifts would make up for all the work and commotion.

They made good time and were able to reach the little hamlet of Dixonville, which was about 35 miles north of Peace River. They decided to stay there overnight to rest the horses and then carry on first thing in the morning. They had soup and sandwiches for supper at the same place they had found lodging for the evening. The people who owned the little lodge were gracious and kind and made them feel right at home. They had a very pleasant evening visiting with different people who were also travelling, including a young couple with a boy Brodie's age. The lad enjoyed having someone to play with for the evening rather than sitting around and being bored with old folks. The father of the young family, Brent, played the guitar and everyone enjoyed a few Christmas carols and some glasses of bubbly Christmas spirits.

Morning came too soon for Carson, who had stayed up late – and maybe had one Christmas cheer too many. He groaned when Bev shook him awake. Knowing he wouldn't get much sympathy from his good wife, he rolled reluctantly out of the warm bed.

Soon they were all loaded back into the sleigh. Waving goodbye to everyone and bidding all a Merry Christmas, they headed out onto the trail. They were about 10 miles from North Star when they saw two men on horseback coming toward them on the winding trail. As they met, Carson wished them a Merry Christmas and, to his horror, one of the men pulled a pistol from beneath his coat.

"Stop the team, Mister."

Carson, keeping his eyes on the gun, pulled the team to a stop. Bev grabbed Carson's arm with one hand and reached to pull Brodie to her with the other, trying to shield him with her body. Carson said, "What's your problem, mister? What do you want?"

The man with the gun said, "Shut up and just do what you're told."

He motioned to the other man and said, "You follow behind."

There was nothing about the two men that had given Carson any warning that they were up to no good when he first saw them. If there had been, he would have made a run for it. Now, facing a loaded gun, he didn't have much choice but to do what he'd been told.

The older man was scruffy, unkempt and unshaven, while the younger one was just the opposite. Wearing clean clothes and with a clean-shaven face, he was not bad looking, Carson thought to himself. Why would a young, good-looking kid hang around with the likes of that old troublemaker? He was probably too lazy to work. Carson knew in his heart that they were going to rob them.

Carson shook his head in disgust and clicked to the team to follow the older man wherever he was taking them. They travelled for about five miles back into the bush until they came to a rundown shack that didn't have a window that hadn't been smashed out. Motioning for the people on the sleigh to get off, they herded them into the old shack. Hollering at Brodie to get some firewood, they took the couple into the shack and tied Carson to a chair. Not recognizing Brodie for the spunky little boy he was, they thought he wouldn't run away because of the old people. But the young boy ran.

When the boy didn't come back with the wood the younger man went to see where he was. Cussing and swearing, and realizing the boy had taken off, the man jumped on his horse to see if he could catch him.

Brodie, in the meantime, knowing they would try to follow his footprints, ran as hard as he could and then stopped to break off a pine branch. Struggling to break it, he began to cry when at first he couldn't rip it from the tree. Slowing himself, he reached into his pocket for his jack-knife. He knew not to cut the branch where they would see it so he ran around to the other side of the tree and hacked off a branch. Reaching down to where he had walked, he brushed his footprints out of the snow. Next he took off running backwards for a couple hundred feet and then brushed his prints away again. Taking off another way, still running backwards, he hoped to confuse the men looking for him into thinking that he was going toward them.

He came to a creek bank with lots of brush and, sitting on his bum, he slid down the bank into the ravine. As he sat at the bottom he noticed a hole in the bank. Crawling up, he crept into the den knowing it was probably a bear's den. Being raised in the wilderness and going hunting a lot with his Dad, Brodie knew he was taking a terrible chance crawling into the hole. But if he was going to save himself, he had no choice.

The young outlaw followed the footprints trying to figure out where the kid had gone, but couldn't see him anywhere and returned to the cabin. When he entered the cabin he said to the older man, "I couldn't find him, but the weather will stop him. It's getting colder and the snow is deep so he won't get too far."

Brodie, lying in the bear den, was out of the cold. It was actually quite warm in the cave. He lay patiently in one place listening to the big black bear breathing about ten feet away from him. Once darkness fell he would try to find his way back to the old shack and Carson and Bev.

The younger man brought in the wood and hollered at Bev to make them something to eat with supplies they had brought in from the sleigh. Bev watched as they went through the Christmas presents, unwrapping and snooping through all the gifts for her family. She was so mad she felt like taking the big frying pan and hitting them over their heads, but as long as Carson was tied to the chair she didn't dare do anything heroic. Actually, Carson, watching her, wouldn't have put it past her. He knew exactly what she was thinking and that she wasn't one to mess with when she was mad. The biggest find the two men discovered was the two bottles of rum packed in the sleigh. Carson, still watching Bev, was feeling proud of her for not losing her cool as she fixed the fire and started making a meal.

Laughing, the men poured themselves some drinks into dirty cups from the cupboard. Sitting down, they waited for their food, talking and joking as if the old couple weren't there. Bev fixed a plate and took it over to Carson. She was going to feed him and then have some herself when the older outlaw knocked the plate from her hand. When the plate hit the floor he stomped on it with his boot and said, "No food for nobody except us."

Bev wanted to slap his sneering face, but looking at the evil in the man's eyes she said, "Fine! Get it yourself then!" and walked over to Carson.

Carson held his breath and wondered what was going to happen, but the outlaw just laughed and said, "I'll just do that."

Sitting down beside Carson, she reached over and put her hand on his knee and said, "We'll get out of here somehow."

As the men drank, they hollered at Bev to go split more wood and bring it in for the night. She split what she thought would last the night, all the while trying to see if she could spot Brodie anywhere, but there was no sign of the little boy. She cried because it was getting so cold and she was afraid that the little boy was going to freeze to death. Packing in the wood, she filled the old stove with as much as she could and then piled the rest beside it. The older man grunted and got up. He pushed Bev roughly into a chair and tied her up too. As the bottles of rum disappeared, the men got more stupid and drunk, laughing hysterically at their own jokes. Finally, their bellies couldn't hold anymore and they fell asleep or passed out. As the evening wore on, the lamp went out and the two old people sat tied together in the dark.

Meanwhile, back in the den, Brodie had fallen asleep. When he woke he couldn't believe that he had actually fallen asleep with a bear, but he had. Wiggling himself from the den, he was happy to see that it wasn't snowing. Now he had to find his way back to the cabin to see if he could help Carson and Bev. The moon was shining down on the glistening snow making it easy for Brodie to find his way back to the cabin. He was surprised to discover that he had run as far as he had through the deep snow. Reaching the shack, he couldn't see any lights on. He soon found a broken window close to where he had seen them push Carson down. Hoisting himself up, he listened to see if he could hear any voices. The only sound was the snoring of the two outlaws.

Carson spotted a head silhouetted in the moonlight. He motioned to Bev not to make any noise. Brodie climbed slowly in the window without making a sound and crept over to Carson. He knelt down beside him and cut the ropes with his jack-knife. Once Carson was free he released Bev. Creeping to the window, they helped Bev through and then Brodie helped Carson, which was difficult with the older man's broken leg.

As soon as he had the couple safely out, Brodie looked around the room. In the semi darkness he could see the presents thrown everywhere. He crept around picking them up and throwing them out the window. Carson just wanted him to get out of there – the hell with all those damn presents! The kid was going to get himself killed. Carson and Bev made trip after trip to the sleigh with the gifts, throwing them into the back of the sleigh. On Carson's last trip to the sleigh he lifted up the seat and pulled out his rifle and then went back to the window. What was that kid doing now? One part of Carson was so proud of the little boy, but the other part was terrified that he would get caught. Finally, Brodie appeared in the window with something wrapped in a blanket. What did he have now? Carson pulled the parcel through the window and then half-lifted Brodie through to safety. Once they were away from the cabin Carson asked, "What's in this blanket?"

Brodie, tucking a pistol inside his coat, said, "All of Grandma Bev's food and candies – they're not getting it! I've got their gun too. Now they can't shoot us."

"Well," Carson replied, "You can give me the gun once we're out of here." Brodie nodded his head.

The outlaws had not bothered with the team and had left the poor horses harnessed to the sleigh. This turned out to be a lucky break for the little family. After moving the horses slowly along, they all began to breathe easier the farther they got from the shack and the drunken men. Carson drove with his rifle across his lap. Brodie and Bev were crouched down in the back of the sleigh. They had spent most of the night in the shack and Carson was surprised to find that it was almost morning.

They were two miles from North Star when they heard riders coming. Carson knew immediately that it was the outlaws, but, by damn, he was ready for them this time – he had his rifle and they had no gun, or so he thought. Bev cried out in fear as they came sweeping toward them. Carson hollered at Brodie to climb up beside him and said, "Take the reins and keep going no matter what."

They could hear the men hollering at them to stop and nobody was more surprised than Carson when he heard a shot being fired. Brodie's heart stopped. Why hadn't he searched for another gun and why hadn't he chased their horses away? Another shot came at them, barely whizzing over their heads. These men weren't only criminals, they were killers. Carson raised his rifle and aimed. He pulled the trigger and saw one of the men fall, hitting the ground hard. That didn't stop the other gunman. He fired at the sleigh again and hit the front of it, narrowly missing Brodie's leg. As the wood splintered, Bev heard Carson swear – nobody could swear like Carson. Mad as a hornet, he swung around and fired again at the oncoming horseman. Hearing a click Brodie knew immediately that Carson's rifle had jammed.

The outlaw was coming alongside the sleigh now. Carson was fighting to get the shell out. Knowing it was going to be too late, he launched himself out of the sleigh at the man on the horse. He knocked the man from the horse and they both fell to the ground. The minute Brodie realized Carson had jumped out of the sleigh he started to pull the running team to a stop. Watching the men rolling on the ground, he heard Carson groan and knew he must have hurt his broken leg. The scruffy man got to his feet first and pointed his gun at Carson's head, saying, "You should have stayed put."

Brodie's heart was pounding as he pulled the robber's pistol from his coat. He had forgotten about the gun in all the excitement. With trembling hands, the boy raised the gun and pulled the trigger. Two shots rang out simultaneously and Brodie watched the gunman fall on top of Carson.

Screaming, Bev scrambled out of the sleigh and ran toward Carson. Bev could see Carson pushing the wounded man off of him. Somehow Brodie had managed to wound the outlaw but hadn't killed him. Not that Bev cared at this point if he was dead or not, but she was grateful for the brave youngster's sake. Helping her husband up, tears blinding her eyes, Bev said, "Oh God … I thought he killed you."

"He dammed near did," Carson said as he pointed to the ground where the bullet had gone into the snow right beside where his head had been, "but I'm okay." He stumbled in the direction of the young boy who was coming slowly toward them. Carson took the gun from Brodie's trembling hand and the boy buried his face into Carson's coat.

"I thought he killed you ... I thought you were dead," he sobbed out.

"I thought I was too, Brodie. You saved my life, but I think I've broken my dammed leg again. It hurts like hell." Carson went on, "Brodie, I need you to help me go back and check on that young man to see if I killed him. I hope I didn't, but if I did you will have to help me load him onto his horse. This guy's lucky – you only hit him in the back of his shoulder. I think it's broken but he won't be going anywhere. Run back to the sleigh and get my rifle. Bev, you're going to stay here and watch this fella," he said as he handed the pistol to her and pointed to the gunman on the ground.

When Brodie returned with the rifle, Carson removed the jammed shell and put in a new one saying, "Okay, Brodie, let's go, and, Bev, if he even twitches, shoot him."

Brodie led the outlaw's horse over to Carson, who held onto the bridle for support and started back toward the man on the trail. Carson was glad to find the man alive though in bad shape, the bullet having entered his chest. Well, Carson thought, I guess that's where I aimed. The man was unconscious and blood was bubbling from his lips. Carson figured the bullet must have pierced the man's lung and hoped they could get him into town before the young man died – he wasn't too keen on killing anyone.

Bev stood watching the outlaw on the ground and said, "Why? Why did you do this? Why would you want to hurt or, better still, why would you want to kill somebody? We would have shared our food with you if you were hungry. If you were broke, Carson would have given you some money." Then Bev got mad. "If you had killed my husband, you would have left five grandchildren without a grandfather. I would have no husband and my children no father! His parents are very old and this would have destroyed them. Don't you know that when someone dies it's not only the one that's dead that's affected, but also everyone that person leaves behind? Maybe you'll die here by yourself in the cold. Do you have anybody that cares if you live or die? I won't be comforting you if you die in front of me. I have no tenderness in my heart toward you, but if you still have a mother … I would find it in my heart to try and comfort her."

The outlaw closed his eyes tightly as pain racked his body. He supposed she was right; he could bleed to death out here by himself if they chose not to help him. He guessed that was their right because he had been planning to dispatch them. If he could only get the gun from her, he'd still shoot her.

Bev was surprised to see a rider coming from another direction. As the rider got closer, he somehow looked familiar in the way he sat on his horse. That's strange, Bev thought, who would she know way out here? The tilt of the man's hat and the way he held his shoulders was definitely that of someone she knew. Bev gasped as the rider came closer.

"Brian! My God, is that you?" she cried. Before her was her long-gone son-in-law. Staggering back up against a tree and looking up at the man on the horse, she said, "My God, Brian, where have you come from?"

Swinging down off his horse, the black-eyed, good-looking man said, "Bev, what the hell's going on here?" He strode over to her and hugged her. Taking the pistol from her trembling hands, he said, "I'll take this before you shoot me or yourself in the foot."

"Brian, where did you come from? How did you get here? Where are you going?"

"Slow down, slow down, woman! First, tell me what's going on here."

Bev quickly told him and then said, "Carson shot another man back there, down the trail, and he went back to get him."

Brian handed the gun back to Bev and said, "Be careful. I'll go see if he needs help." Swinging himself back on his horse, he said to the man on the ground, "I'm glad it's you she's pointing that gun at and not me." He turned the horse around and headed down the trail to find his father-in-law.

Farther down the trail he discovered the young boy holding a horse while the older man was trying to lift the dead weight of an unconscious man on the ground. Brian leapt off his horse, a beautiful black high-strung animal. Brodie thought he had never in his life seen such a good-looking horse. In fact, the man and horse seemed a good match, as if they were made for each other.

"Hello, Carson," the man said. "Need a hand?" Carson, recognizing the voice, dropped the man to the ground and swung around.

"Brian," he hollered, "Is that you?" Stumbling, he held his arms out to greet his son-in-law, whom he hadn't seen in two years, but his strength failed him and he collapsed to the ground.

"Lord, man!" Brian said. "Were you shot in the leg?"

"No," Carson moaned. "I broke my leg six months ago and I think I just broke the damn thing again."

Brian helped the older man stand up and said; "I don't think you could have lifted this fella up onto the horse by yourself."

"No," Carson said, "I thought Brodie could help me, but it's all he can do to hold the horse. I was just going to send him back for Bev and the sleigh. Did you see her?"

"Yes," said Brian, "And the mood she's in we'd better hurry and load this bistard before she shoots that other 'bistard'." Brian didn't like to hear anybody cussing so he usually made up his own swear words. Carson had to laugh – it had been a long time since had heard that word. In fact, he hadn't heard it since the last time he had seen Brian. His son-in-law's unique swear words always gave him a chuckle. There was no doubt in his mind or in Brian's exactly what Bev would do if the guy moved. Yes, he was married to a pretty feisty lady. And both he and Brian had been a time or two on the wrong end of a tongue-lashing.

When Brian had the wounded man on the horse, he helped Carson get on behind to hold the unconscious man. Groaning in pain, Carson lifted his injured leg over the horse's back. When he was settled Brian led the horse over to his mount and swung back into the saddle, then looked down at the white-faced little boy standing beside him and asked, "What's your name, boy?"

"I'm Brodie," the little boy answered. "Sir, I'm a friend of Morgan, Sydnee, and Rachel. I don't think Ashley likes me … she calls me a bad boy and a dumb-dumb all the time. I came to help Carson and Bev, but I don't think I'm doing a very good job."

"Brodie," Carson said, "How can you say such a thing? You saved my life twice already!" He proceeded to tell Brian how Brodie had helped them escape from the shack and how he had gone back for the presents. He went on, "If all that wasn't enough, that other fellow up there was going to shoot me, but Brodie shot him first. The only reason I wasn't killed was because Brodie fired and threw that other guy off balance. His bullet went into the ground right beside my head – two inches the other way I would have been a dead man."

"God, you poor kid!" Brian said, turning to Brodie, "You handled things as well as any grown man. What more could you have done?"

"I should have run their horses off at the shack," Brodie replied, "And none of this would have happened."

Extending his hand to Brodie, Brian said, "Come on, I'll give you a ride to the sleigh on my horse. For some reason Black loves kids. Then we'd better hurry back to Grandma. I wouldn't want to be that outlaw. Can you imagine the lecture he's getting?" Brodie had to laugh. He knew Grandma Bev well. He and Morgan had been in that outlaw's place a time or two, minus the gun.

Bev saw them coming and heaved a sigh of relief. She said, "Let's tidy the back of the sleigh and then we can load these two back there."

Leaving Carson on the back of the horse, Bev and Brian hastily rewrapped presents and neatly stacked everything into place. That done, Brian said, "Bev, are you going to try to stop them from bleeding to death once I get them loaded?"

"Yes, I will, but you have to stay close. I don't trust that fellow there on the ground."

They unloaded the man from Carson's horse and onto the sleigh first. Bev worked quickly to press a towel against the man's chest. With Brian's help she tied a ripped bed sheet around the man's torso to keep the towel tightly in place. Brian looked up at Carson on the horse and asked, "Are you okay up there or do you want down?"

"No," said Carson, "I'm okay as long as I don't move so I'll just stay where I am."

When they were finished with the young criminal Brian hopped down from the sleigh and went to the scruffy man on the ground. Grabbing the man none-too-gently by the collar, he hauled the outlaw to his feet. "Get up, you bistard," he said and pushed him toward the sleigh.

Groaning, the man crawled into the back of the sleigh and said to Bev, "Are you going to let me bleed to death?"

"I've got a good notion to," she replied. "You were the one doing all the shooting. You meant to kill us and, what's worse, you would have killed this boy too if you had the chance."

When they had made the outlaw comfortable they started out on the last two miles to the little town ahead. Carson remained on his horse thinking he could make it and not wanting to move his leg again if he didn't have to.

Brian let Brodie ride Black. The young boy was ecstatic to be riding the big horse by himself. Brian drove the sleigh and team with Bev sitting in the back of the sleigh holding the young outlaw's head in her lap. She felt sorry for the young criminal. How did one so young get mixed up with someone like the killer sitting beside her?

When they reached the town Brian headed to the doctor's office with Carson leading the way. The doctor came out and they helped Carson off the horse.

"Carson, it's nice to see you again. What have you done to yourself this time?" It was the same doctor who had set his leg when he had fallen off the ladder at Lana's.

Brian told him what had happened and then said, "He thinks he broke it again. Can you help him? He's in a lot of pain. These two aren't going anyplace," he said motioning to the men in the sleigh. "I'll go find the sheriff and they can help me with them."

Bev and Brodie hurried into the doctor's office with the doctor and Carson. They helped Carson out of his heavy clothes and the doctor examined the bruised and scraped leg. He said, "You're lucky, Carson. It isn't broken, but you sure gave it a beating." The leg was beginning to swell and was throbbing. Carson put his head into his hands. The doctor said, "I'll give you something for pain and you'll be okay in about 20 minutes."

The door opened behind them as Brian and the RCMP officer hauled in the unconscious man. "Put him over there on that table," the doctor said. He helped Carson off the examining table and assisted him to the bed where Bev fussed over him.

Seeing the scruffy man, the officer said, "Well ... somebody finally caught up with you, Frank. You and Ben have been on the run a long time terrorizing people. Until now no one had any evidence on the two of you but it looks like we have some live witnesses for a change. You two have had this coming for a long time."

Bev turned around and said incredulously, "You mean they've done this to folks before?"

"Yes," said the officer. "We've been after them for a long time. We believe they have robbed and beaten people and even left them to die from their wounds, but this is the first time that I know of that they tried to shoot a family."

Bev turned on the man and said, "You're damn lucky I didn't know about this first or I would have let you bleed to death. You really are the scum of the earth." The scruffy, hardened man cringed as he came eye to eye with the angry grandma.

Once everyone had settled down, Brian asked the RCMP officer if he knew where Lana lived so he could go get her and his girls. The doctor said, "She's not home. She went to be with her brother and children for Christmas."

"What do you mean? Weren't the children in town with her?"

"No," the doctor said. "They've been with her brother for the last two months while she got her business going and fixed up a home for those little girls."

Brian hung his head. So his life had come to this … well … maybe he could make some amends. There was no doubt that it would take time to fix the mistakes he made in his life. The young couple had separated after not getting along. He had joined the army and found himself fighting a war for the United States. He had seen a lot of bad things and had been part of circumstances he wasn't proud of. But he was happy that he was still alive. Many men he had known weren't. His biggest desire now was to find a job, meet up with his little girls, and help make a life for them.

It was now the afternoon of the 24th and Carson said, "Doc, do you think you could give me enough painkillers so that I can make the rest of the trip?"

The doctor nodded his head and said, "While I'm at it, I'm going to ask my wife to fix something for us to eat. A bit of a rest won't hurt and then you can be on your way."

When everyone had eaten, rested, and thanked the doctor and the policeman, the little group set out for the cabin and their children. It was one o'clock by the time they got going; it would take them until morning, travelling through the night, to go the 45 miles. Stopping frequently through the night to rest the tired horses, they made their way through the heavy snow. At nine o'clock they stopped and made a fire and had something to eat. The hot tea and meatballs from a jar spread on some bread filled their stomachs. Then pulling themselves from the warmth of the fire, they reorganized the sleigh and started on their way again.

Carson lay in the back of the sleigh where he could rest his leg. Bev and Brian sat in front with Brian driving the team. Brodie was bringing up the rear, riding on Brian's horse, happy as a lark. Every once in awhile Brian would have to ask Carson if they were going the right way or get directions.

As the night wore on the snow got deeper and harder, so Brian jerry-rigged another harness from rope and tied his horse to the front of the two horses pulling the sleigh. The snow was now very deep and the team was all but played out. However, with his horse helping to pull the sleigh, they found they could keep going. When the moon went behind a cloud Carson said, "Help me get in front. You've never been out here before and I don't want us to get lost and lose more time." At five in the morning they came into a clearing and Carson announced, "It's still totally dark, but we're only about half-a-mile from the cabin."

Brian's heart thumped in his chest. Would his family be glad to see him or would they turn him away? Carson sensed what the man was thinking and said, "Your girls will be glad to see you, especially Sydnee. Rachel talks about you, but I don't know if she remembers you … she was only four when you left. And Ashley's quite a character. She picks up on anything you say."

As they pulled up to the cabin, they could see smoke rising straight up into the cold air. It had to be 40 or 50 degrees below zero. A light went on in the cabin. Someone must be a light sleeper if the crunching of the sleigh on the snow had awakened him. The door opened and a handsome young man stood silhouetted in the doorway.

Coming outside with a lantern, the angel held it high in the air and said, "Hello, folks, what in heaven's name are you doing out on a night like this? The only one that should be out tonight is Santa Claus!" The small frozen group agreed with him. Gabriel spotted the young boy in the sleigh and said, "Brodie, is that you? Carson, Bev, Brian, hello! Come in, come in!"

The four people looked at each other. How did this man know them when they had never laid eyes on him until this very minute? Brian said, "I need help getting Carson out of the sleigh. He has a broken leg."

Gabriel said, "Just hang on a moment while I wake Joseph and put on my coat." He disappeared into the cabin before they could ask where Darren was. He was soon back, followed by an old man in a ragged cloak. Meeting his eyes, Bev thought she had never seen such kind eyes in her whole life.

The sound of the men helping Carson into the cabin woke Lana. Grabbing her housecoat, she put it on and opened the curtain. The first thing she saw was her husband helping her father to a chair. "Brian! My God, where did you come from? Daddy, what are you doing here? What's happening?" Running to her husband, she hugged him, exclaiming, "Oh, it's so good to see you! I thought you might be dead." Hearing her mother's voice, she turned around, "Oh, Momma, you're here too! How wonderful. Come in, come in to the fire." A little boy poked his head from behind Bev; "Brodie, come in, honey, and get warm."

Brian went back outside. Well, she hadn't kicked him out. That was a good sign. He rejoined the men and helped them unload the sleigh. Once done, they took the tired animals and made room in the barn for them, feeding them some grain. The men rubbed down the cold horses and packed water from the house for them. Chores done, they walked back to the cabin in silence to be greeted with the happy family reunion going on inside.

As Brian entered the cabin, his eyes fell on his three little girls who had woken up. Sydnee flew into his arms as she recognized him and realized that what she was seeing was real. "Daddy, Daddy!" she screamed as she launched herself into her father's arms. Brian held his oldest daughter in his arms and wept as he hugged her to him. Looking over her shoulder, he put his hand out to Rachel. Shyly, the spunky little girl walked over to him.

"You're my dad and I remember now what you look like." Everyone had to laugh as she too was lifted up into her father's arms.

Ashley, already in her Uma's arms, was arguing with her grandpa, telling him, "It's *my* Uma."

"No," said her grandpa, "That's *my* Uma, you little dummy."

Gabriel looked at Brittany and Morgan and said, "So that's where she got that saying."

They all had to laugh again when Brian set Sydnee and Rachel down and walked over to his baby. "Hi," he said. "Do you want to come to me? I'm your Daddy."

"No!" said the cute little girl who looked so much like him. Cuddling up against her grandma, she said, "Me, no you. Go away you bad boy, you dumb-dumb."

Grandma Bev, shocked, said, "Ashley, you can't talk like that!"

Gabriel said, "Oh, yes, she can. She's called me a bad boy and a dumb-dumb ever since I got here. I can't figure out why she never calls Joseph a dumb-dumb though."

Holding her arms out, the little girl smiled at Gabriel and went into his arms and hugged him. She held his face in her two little hands and looked right into his face. "You nice boy now?" she asked.

Gabriel turned with her toward Brian. "This is your daddy. Can you say hello?"

Knowing that she was the centre of attention, she said to her father, "Hi bad boy." Giving up, everyone left her on her own to make friends with her daddy.

When things had settled down and everyone was introduced to each other, Bev said, "Where are Darren and Alison? Have they gone visiting somewhere?"

"No, Grandma," Brittany replied, "They were in an accident and got badly hurt. They are staying with a man called Nick. Nick has been looking after them and he's supposed to be bringing them home today. Oh, Grandma, I have so much to tell you about what's been going on around here."

While Bev and Lana made breakfast the story unfolded, each child telling his or her own tale. The grownups couldn't believe their ears, hearing what the children had endured. Brian walked over to Brittany and hugged her, with tears in his eyes. "Thank you for saving our little girl. That was pretty brave."

"That's okay, Uncle Brian. Mostly I was afraid of what my mom would say if I had let anything happen to the kids."

Brian hugged her again and laughed, "I think this is one time your mom would be speechless. She would be proud of you."

❆ ❆ ❆

Nick woke Darren and Alison early in the morning, knocking on their door and saying, "Get ready ... we'll be leaving in an hour. The sleigh and reindeer are waiting – they are a bit tired after their busy night, but by the time we're ready to go they'll be fine."

Darren and Alison gave each other the look again. This man seemed so familiar … what was it about him? They dressed as quickly as their condition allowed and ate the breakfast Ava brought to them. She helped them gather their few belongings and then led them to the front door, where she helped them with their coat and cloak. While helping Alison on with hers, Ava said, "It was nice having you here, my dear. I'm going to miss you."

Hugging her, Alison replied, "Thank you for helping me. I know I wouldn't be alive if it weren't for your care."

The door opened and Nick stood there in a red coat. Alison laughed and said, "Well I guess we can't lose you in that bright red coat!"

Nick joined in the laughter, enjoying their amusement over his red coat. "Well," he announced, "It *is* Christmas Day."

The sleigh and reindeer stood out front and Darren said, "Nick, where did you get your reindeer?"

"Oh, at the North Pole, but they're a little different from your ordinary reindeer."

"How so?" Alison asked as Nick and Darren lifted her into the sleigh.

"Oh, they're magical," Nick said. Again Darren and Alison laughed; they so enjoyed Nick's sense of humour.

"Look," said Darren to Alison, "Nick went back to the accident site and picked up all of our belongings. He even found my rifle."

"Yes, son, and I don't think there's much wrong with your sleigh. In the spring you can probably pull it out of there and take it home."

"Good," said Darren as he settled himself on the seat beside Alison in the huge sleigh. Ava stood on the porch waving. Alison threw a kiss back at her. Then, to her astonishment, elves in red and green attire appeared everywhere! Darren and Alison screamed with glee when quaint cottage-style houses started appearing everywhere.

Nick said, "See those long cottages in rows? They are the workshops of the elves. That's where the elves make toys for children all over the world. Welcome to the North Pole! This is where you have been since you arrived at our home."

As Nick took the reins in his hands, a Santa Claus hat the same colour as his coat appeared on his head, a black belt appeared around his girth and his boots turned black. Golden snowflakes fell from the sky around him and a beautiful yellow light shone over the whole village, illuminating everything. He actually was Santa Claus! Darren and Alison laughed aloud with wonderment, hugging each other. They were indeed at the North Pole and they were sitting in Santa Claus's sleigh. Either they were asleep and dreaming or they were hallucinating, but they knew they couldn't both be having the same dream.

Santa announced, "Are you ready?"

They could only nod their heads and wave to all their new friends as the reindeer took to the air, pulling the sleigh with them. Santa flew over the village so they could fill their eyes with the fairytale of the North Pole below them. Never had they seen anything so wonderful, flying above the trees and looking down at everything on the ground. They were indeed part of a wonderful miracle and blessed to be in the presence of Santa Claus. This was something they had always thought of as a fairy tale, but somehow it was as real as being alive.

Within 10 minutes they were at the cabin, landing on the roof. The reindeer stamped and pranced until all those inside the cabin ran out to see what was making all the noise. When everyone was outside, standing with open mouths, Santa urged the reindeer off the roof and onto the ground. Lana kept shaking her head, feeling somehow that she was still sleeping and dreaming. As it was not yet daylight, the moon and stars added to the beauty of the moment.

"Joseph," Lana whispered to the old man standing beside her. "What's happening? Am I awake?"

The children were laughing and screaming with excitement. Brittany and Morgan were hugging and kissing and crying in the arms of their mother and father. The bells on the reindeer were jingling, adding to the madness. Madness or bliss, Lana's legs could no longer hold her up so she sat down on the step, trying to take in everything. Carson and Bev stood holding each other – they had lived long enough to witness a miracle.

Bev helped Carson over to greet Darren and Alison. Crying, they told their children how grateful they were that they were alive.

"Santa Claus," Lana said in wonder. "I haven't believed in him since I was a child." She rubbed her eyes, but when she opened them they were still all there. Pushing herself to her feet, she said, "Come, come in and have some breakfast. We were just finishing up. We have lots of food and we haven't yet opened our presents. Let's go in and enjoy this wonderful moment."

Once inside, Ashley promptly set herself on Santa Claus's lap and said, "Me like you. You good boy."

Santa laughed and said, "Me like you too, Ashley. I've heard a lot about you."

Everyone opened gifts while Santa Claus ate breakfast. Joseph looked grand in his new floor-length cloak. The children's toys from Joseph and Gabriel were wonderful. There was a huge rocking horse for the little girls and a beautiful jewellery box for Brittany. An angel made from wood stood in the centre of the box and turned when the music played. Never had any of them seen anything so exquisite or so interesting. For Morgan they had built a bike with wooden wheels and pedals that turned to make the bike drive. It was wonderful. For Lana, Alison, and Bev there were beautiful Bibles with white bindings. For Darren, they had built a train set to share with Morgan. You could wind it up with a key to make it go. For Carson and Brian there were hunting knives. Where they had come from only God knew. Brian wondered how they knew to have presents for him when Brian himself didn't know he was going to be here for Christmas. Carson and Bev were wondering the same thing as they had just arrived that morning and no one had known they were coming. Brodie stood holding his gift, a bow and arrow set. It was just what he wanted. Morgan had one too.

The only present yet to be opened was Gabriel's when Santa said, "I hate to rush everyone, but it's time for us to go."

"What do you mean?" Darren asked.

Santa said, "Joseph, Gabriel, and I have to leave soon."

"But I haven't had a chance to get to know Joseph and Gabriel yet," Darren said. "And I haven't thanked anyone."

"What do you mean Joseph has to leave?" Lana asked. "Joseph isn't going anywhere. He's going to stay with me."

"Everyone, please sit down," Santa said. "We have a story to tell you."

When everyone was settled Santa said, "I want you to know who these men really are. Lana, this is Saint Joseph. He came from heaven to help you and he really is the carpenter Joseph. He truly is Jesus' earthly Father. You needed help and God the Father heard your prayers." Before Lana's eyes, Joseph's new cloak turned into the same beautiful blue that she had seen in her dream.

"Oh, Joseph, how wonderful," she said as a golden glow radiated like a halo over the old man's head.

"Darren, Alison, Lana, Bev, Carson, and kids, meet Gabriel."

"Gabriel, open your present and put it on," Santa went on. Gabriel opened the gift and pulled the silvery-white sweater over his golden head. Silvery-white glowing angel wings sprouted from his back immediately. The span and the beauty of the huge wings were beyond the imagination. Everyone stood not daring to move for fear the beautiful angel might disappear.

"Oh, my God!" Lana blurted out. "You truly were our children's guardian angel, God's messenger straight from heaven. How wonderful! Oh, Gabriel, please forgive me for being so closed when you and the children told me that you were an angel."

Gabriel smiled and said, "There is nothing to forgive, but from now on don't be afraid to believe – angels truly do walk the face of the earth."

Santa said, "Yes, we were sent by heaven to help you all through your ordeals. We know life is hard and every once in awhile we get to help a whole family. We must go because our help is needed now in other places."

The children flew into Gabriel's arms crying, "Don't go! Please, don't go. We'll be good and help out as much as we can. Stay with us!"

Gabriel comforted them, telling them that even though they wouldn't be able to see him, he would always be close to them because he was their guardian angel.

Morgan said, "We'll never forget how wonderful you are. Say Hi to Jesus for us."

Gabriel nodded his head, "I will, but I don't have to – for He hears every word you say."

Gabriel looked down at Ashley, who was pulling on his leg. Bending down, he scooped her up into his arms. He lifted her off the floor and flew around the room with her, being careful not to hit or knock anything over with his huge wings. Of course, Ashley wasn't the only one who was spellbound. Resting on the floor once more, she held his face with her little hands so that he could look only at her and said, "Ashee like you. You not dumb-dumb."

Gabriel kissed the top of her little head and said, "Me love you too."

Lana was crying in Joseph's arms. "Oh, Joseph, it has been such a long time since I have felt loved and safe with someone. You have taken such wonderful care of me. Whatever will I do without you?"

Joseph said, "I promise you, Lana, someone will either come home to stay and take his place with your family or else one heck of a good man will turn up for you. God is watching and He doesn't mean for you to be alone." Brian met the old man's eyes and knew that whatever the future brought, he would try his best.

Darren stood with his hand in Santa's and said, "I feel like a lost little boy. I have just found the most wonderful friend in the world and now I'm going to lose him."

"No, Darren, every year on the Saviour's birthday think of me and I'll be in your dreams for the night."

The three men went outside with the little family following, everyone hugging and kissing farewell to each other. Once again Gabriel had Ashley in his arms. Climbing into the sleigh with the little girl, he said, "Is Ashley coming with me?"

She solemnly looked at him and said, "No, me stay with Daddy." She held her little arms out to Brian and Gabriel gently placed her in her father's arms.

Bev felt a small hand sliding into hers. She looked down at Brodie standing beside her, his eyes as big as saucers. "I'll never forget this as long as I live, will I, Grandma Bev?"

"No, honey, you'll always be able to tell this story," she said as she reached down to hug the man in the little boy's body.

Finally, all three saints were together in the sleigh, and the children and adults stood in a little group watching the reindeer pull the sleigh into the mid-morning dawn. The stars were fading from the night sky as the sleigh circled the cabin a few times and then the three saints disappeared into the emerging dawn.

The family stood with their arms around one another, tears falling. They had much to talk about and much to celebrate. Never had a family felt so wonderful or been blessed by so much. Each and every one of them felt humbled. They walked into the cabin to enjoy their Christmas Day and, more importantly, to celebrate that they were once again a happy united family.

They had many tales to tell over the years; each one had a miracle to tell. Never again did they doubt the existence of St. Nicholas, St. Joseph, or the angel Gabriel. It was a Christmas story to be told over and over again until the end of their days.

Merry Christmas to all and God bless everyone, especially my grandma for sharing this story with me.

Author Biography

Beverly Lein was born in Manning, Alberta, and grew up in nearby Sunny Valley on her father's farm. Before raising elk with her husband Carson on their farm, she worked as a clerk, ran a confectionary store, farmed, and did the secretarial work in the Shell Bulk Station that she and her husband managed for 10 years.

As a mother of two and a grandmother of five, Bev honed her natural-born storyteller's instinct. She spends many late nights and before-dawn mornings writing down her thoughts, fantasies, and storylines. Her grandchildren are her sounding board, her avid critics, and her greatest fans. They still gather 'round to hear how each story turns out.

LaVergne, TN USA
14 October 2009
160771LV00004B/5/P